MASTERPIECE

MASTERPIECE

ELISE BROACH
Illustrated by Kelly Murphy

THORNDIKE PRESS

A part of Gale, Cengage Learning

GALE
CENGAGE Learning

Detroit • New York • San Francisco • New Haven, Conn • Waterville, Maine • London

GALE
CENGAGE Learning

Recommended for Middle Readers.
Text copyright © 2008 by Elise Broach.
Illustrations copyright © 2008 by Kelly Murphy.
Thorndike Press, a part of Gale, Cengage Learning.

Thorndike Press® Large Print The Literacy Bridge.
The text of this Large Print edition is unabridged.
Other aspects of the book may vary from the original edition.
Set in 16 pt. Plantin.
Printed on permanent paper.

LIBRARY OF CONGRESS CATALOGING-IN-PUBLICATION DATA

Broach, Elise.
  Masterpiece/ by Elise Broach ; illustrated by Kelly Murphy.
    p. cm.
  Summary: After Marvin, a beetle, makes a miniature drawing as an eleventh birthday gift for James, a human with whom he shares a house, the two new friends work together to help recover an Albrecht Dürer drawing stolen from the Metropolitan Museum of Art.
  ISBN-13: 978-1-4104-1244-7 (lg. print : hardcover : alk. paper)
  ISBN-10: 1-4104-1244-X (lg. print : hardcover : alk. paper)
  1. Large type books. [1. Artists—Fiction. 2. Beetles—Fiction. 3. Human-animal relationships—Fiction. 4. Art thefts—Fiction. 5. Family life—New York (State)—New York—Fiction. 6. Dürer, Albrecht, 1471-1528—Fiction. 7. New York (N.Y.)—Fiction. 8. Mystery and detective stories. 9. Large type books.]
  I. Murphy, Kelly, 1977– ill. II. Title.
PZ7.B78083Mas 2009
[Fic]—dc22   2008038994

Published in 2009 by arrangement with Henry Holt and Company, LLC.

Printed in the United States of America
1 2 3 4 5 6 7 12 11 10 09 08

For Zoe, Harry, and Grace

"Nobody sees a flower really;
it is so small.
We haven't time,
and to see takes time —
like to have a friend takes time."
— Georgia O'Keeffe

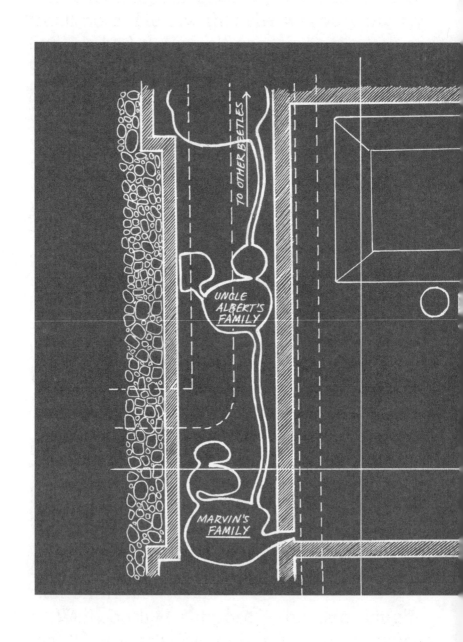

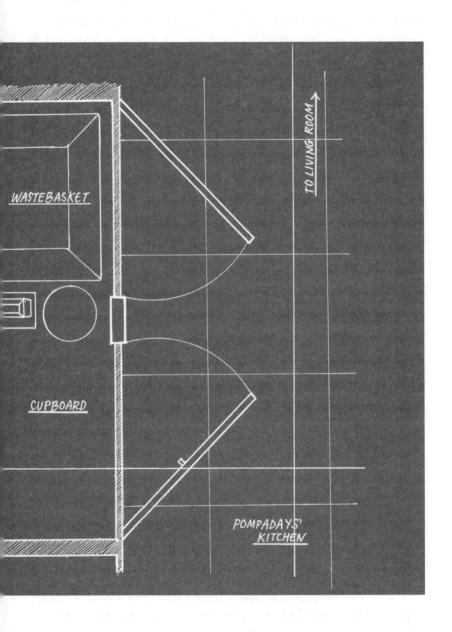

MASTERPIECE

A FAMILY EMERGENCY

Home, for Marvin's family, was a damp corner of the cupboard beneath the kitchen sink. Here, a leaking pipe had softened the plaster and caused it to crumble away. Just behind the wall, Marvin's family had hollowed out three spacious rooms, and, as his parents often remarked, it was a perfect location. It was warm, because of the hot-water pipes embedded in the wall; moist, to make burrowing easy; and dark and musty, like all the other homes the family had lived in. Best of all, the white plastic wastebasket that loomed on one side offered a constant litter of apple cores, bread crumbs, onion skins, and candy wrappers, making the cupboard an ideal foraging ground.

Marvin and his relatives were beetles. They had shiny black shells, six legs, and excellent night vision. They were medium-sized, as beetles go, not much bigger than a raisin. But they were very agile: good at climbing walls, scurrying across counter-tops, and slipping under closed doors. They lived in the large apartment of a human family, the Pompadays, in New York City.

One morning, Marvin awoke to find the household in an uproar. Usually the first sounds of the day were the gentle rustlings of his parents in the next room and, in the distance, the clank of pots in the Pompaday kitchen sink. But today he heard the frantic clicking of Mrs. Pompaday's high heels, and her voice, anxious and shrill. Just as he was beginning to wonder what had happened, his mother came looking for him in a great hurry.

"Marvin!" she cried. "Come quickly, darling! We have an emergency."

Marvin crawled out of the soft cotton ball that was his bed and, still only half-awake, followed her into the living room. There, his father, his uncle Albert, and his cousin Elaine were deep in conversation. Elaine ran to him and grabbed one of his legs.

"Mrs. Pompaday has lost her contact lens! Down the bathroom sink! And since you're

14

the only one who knows how to swim, we need *you* to fish it out!"

Marvin drew back in surprise, but his cousin continued happily. "Oh! What if you drown?"

Marvin was not nearly as thrilled at this prospect as Elaine. "I won't drown," he said firmly. "I'm a good swimmer."

He'd practiced swimming for almost a month now, in an old juice bottle cap filled with water. He was the only member of his entire family who could swim, a skill his parents both marveled at and took credit for.

"Marvin has exceptional coordination, such fine control over his legs," Mama often remarked. "It reminds me of my days in the ballet."

"When he sets his mind to something, there's no stopping him," Papa would add smugly. "He's a chip off the old block."

But right now, these words were little comfort to Marvin. Swimming in a bottle cap was one thing — it was half an inch deep. Swimming inside a drainpipe was something else altogether. He paced the room nervously.

Mama was talking to Uncle Albert, looking mad. "Well, I should think not!" she exclaimed. "He's just a child. I say let the Pompadays call a plumber."

Papa shook his head. "It's too risky. If a plumber goes poking around in there, he'll see that the wall is rotting away. He'll say they need to replace it, and that'll be the end of Albert and Edith's home."

Uncle Albert nodded vigorously and beckoned to Marvin. "Marvin, my boy, what do you say? You'll have to go down the bathroom pipe and find that contact lens. Think you can handle it?"

Marvin hesitated. Mama and Papa were still arguing. Now Papa looked at him unhappily. "I'd go myself, son — you know I would — if I could swim."

"No one can swim like Marvin," Elaine declared. "But even Marvin may not be able to swim well enough. There's probably a lot

of water in that pipe by now. Who knows how far down he'll have to go?" She paused dramatically. "Maybe he'll never make it back up to the surface."

"Hush, Elaine," said Uncle Albert.

Marvin grabbed the fragment of peanut shell that he used as a float when he swam in his own pool at home. He took a deep breath.

"I can try, at least," he said to his parents.

"I'll be careful."

"Then I'm going with you," Mama decided, "to make sure you aren't foolhardy. And if it looks the least bit dangerous, we won't risk it."

And so they set off for the Pompadays' bathroom, with Uncle Albert leading the way. Marvin followed close behind his mother, the peanut shell tucked awkwardly under one of his legs.

DOWN THE DRAIN

It took them a fair bit of time to reach the bathroom. First they had to crawl out of the cupboard into the bright morning light of the Pompadays' kitchen. There, baby William was banging on his high chair with a spoon, scattering Cheerios all over the floor. Ordinarily, the beetles might have waited in the shadows to snatch one and carry it off for lunch, but today there were more important tasks ahead. They scuttled along the baseboard to the living room, and then began the exhausting journey over the Oriental rug, which at least was dark blue, so they didn't have to worry about being seen.

All the way to the bathroom, Marvin could hear Mr. and Mrs. Pompaday yelling at each other.

"I don't understand why you can't just take the pipe apart and find it," Mrs. Pompaday complained. "That's what Karl would have done." Karl was Mrs. Pompaday's first husband.

"*You* take the pipe apart and find it. And flood the bathroom. Then we'll have to replace more than your contact lens," Mr. Pompaday fumed. He stomped to the phone. "I'm calling a plumber."

"Oh, fine," said Mrs. Pompaday. "He'll take all day to get here. I have to leave for work in twenty minutes, and I won't be able to find my way to the door without my contact lenses."

James, Mrs. Pompaday's son from her first marriage, stood in the doorway. He was ten years old, a thin boy with big feet, serious gray eyes, and a scattering of freckles across his cheeks. He would be eleven tomorrow, and Marvin and his family had been trying to think of something nice to do for his birthday, since they infinitely preferred him to the rest of the Pompaday family. He was quiet and reasonable, unlikely to make sudden movements or raise his voice.

Seeing him now, Marvin remembered how James had caught sight of him once, a few weeks ago, when Marvin was dragging home an M&M he'd found for the family dessert. Marvin had been so excited about his good luck that he'd forgotten to stay close to the baseboard. There he was, out in the open sea of cream-colored tile in the kitchen, when James's blue sneaker stopped alongside him. Marvin panicked, dropped the M&M, and ran for his life. But James only crouched down and watched him, never saying a word.

Marvin hadn't told his parents about that particular close call. He'd vowed to himself that he'd be more careful in the future.

Now James shifted thoughtfully on those same blue sneakers. "You could wear your

21

glasses, Mom," he said.

"Oh, fine," said Mrs. Pompaday. "Wear my glasses. Fine. I guess it doesn't matter what I look like when I meet clients. Maybe I should just go to work in my bathrobe."

By this time, Uncle Albert, Marvin, and his mother had reached the door of the bedroom, and the bathroom lay just beyond. Unfortunately, the three humans were effectively blocking the route. Three jittery pairs of feet — one in sneakers, one in high heels, and one in loafers — made it hard to find a safe path.

"Stay close to me," Mama told Marvin. She hurried along the door frame. Dodging the spikes of Mrs. Pompaday's heels, Marvin and Uncle Albert followed.

They made it up the bathroom wall to the sink without mishap. Normally, the light tile would have made them easy targets for a rolled-up newspaper or the bottom of a slipper. But the Pompadays were so engrossed in their argument that they didn't notice three shiny black beetles scrambling onto the sink.

"I'll keep a lookout," Uncle Albert said. "You two go ahead."

Marvin and his mother tumbled and slid down the smooth side of the sink to the drain. They ducked under the silver stopper and stood on the edge of the open pipe, staring into blackness.

Marvin could hear a distant trickling sound. As his eyes adjusted, he saw water, murky and uninviting, a few inches below. He thought of Cousin Elaine's grim prediction and shuddered. Why hadn't his mother taken a firmer stand against this?

"Well . . . here I go," he said to Mama, who promptly grabbed his leg and held fast.

"Now don't do anything rash, darling," she told him. "Go slowly, and come right back to me if it seems dangerous."

"Okay," Marvin promised. He clutched his peanut-shell float and took a deep breath. Then he launched himself into the void.

He barely remembered to shut his eyes before the cold water closed over his head. Pedaling his legs frantically, he came bobbing back up to the surface. The cloudy water tasted vaguely of toothpaste. It smelled horrible.

"Marvin? Marvin, are you all right?" Mama's voice echoed thinly in the pipe.

"I'm fine," he called back.

He swam through the scummy water, which was littered with every nasty thing that might wash down a human's drain: bits of food, hair, slivers of soap. He wanted to throw up.

"Do you see it yet?" his mother called.

"No," Marvin answered. He suddenly realized he had no idea what a contact lens looked like.

Then, as he was about to turn back, he *did* see something: a thin plastic disc, stuck to the side of the pipe. It looked just like the fruit bowl Mama used at home. Out of breath, he shot back up to the surface.

"I found it, Mama!" he yelled.

"Oh, good, darling." His mother breathed a sigh of relief. "Now we'd better hurry, before someone turns on the faucet and washes us both away."

Marvin discovered he couldn't hold on to the contact lens and the peanut shell at the same time. Reluctantly, he let go of his float, took a deep breath, and plunged under the water again.

In the distance, he heard his mother cry, "Marvin! Your float!" But he moved his legs swiftly, unburdened by the peanut shell, and glided down through the dark water. He swam straight to the contact lens and clasped it with his front two legs. Pulling it away from the side of the pipe, he shot quickly back to the surface. Through the lens, he could see his mother, wavy and distorted, looming above him. She'd crawled

down the side of the pipe to the water's edge, beckoning to him.

"Oh, Marvin, thank heavens. You are a wonder, darling. What leg control. I wish my old ballet crowd could see you." She took the lens from him. "Whew! The water smells positively vile. And what a fuss over this little thing! Why, it looks exactly like my fruit bowl."

Holding it gingerly on her back, Mama crawled up the pipe. She scooted under the stopper, with Marvin close behind her, and together they dragged the lens up the side of the sink.

Uncle Albert rushed down to meet them. "By George, you've done it!" he cried. "Marvin, my boy, you're a hero! A hero! Wait till I tell your aunt Edith!"

Marvin beamed modestly. He flexed his legs and shook them dry.

"Let's see, where shall we put it?" Mama asked.

They looked around. "By the faucet, maybe," Marvin suggested. "That way, it won't get washed down the drain again."

They placed the lens near the hot-water handle and dashed behind a green water glass just as James walked into the bathroom.

"After all this trouble, they'd better find it," Mama whispered grimly. Marvin kept his eyes on the contact lens. It glistened in the morning light, a faint blue color.

They could hear Mr. Pompaday on the phone with the plumber. "What's that? Oh, okay, I'll look." He bellowed, "James! Are you in the bathroom? Make yourself useful.

Are the pipes in there copper or galvanized steel?"

James stood at the sink. "I don't know," he said. "But, Mom, I found your contact lens. It's right here by the faucet."

And then what a commotion: Mrs. Pompaday rushing into the bathroom in disbelief, Mr. Pompaday loudly apologizing to the plumber, and James lifting the contact lens in his outstretched palm.

"Well, I guess that's that," Mama said to Marvin as soon as the bathroom emptied. "We'd better head back and let your father know you're all right."

So Mama, Uncle Albert, and Marvin ambled home, where everyone greeted them joyfully. Papa, Aunt Edith, and Elaine all patted Marvin on his shell, but nobody wanted to hug him. He was wet and slimy, and smelled overpoweringly of the drain water.

"I think I need a bath," Marvin said.

And then Mama and Papa fussed over him, filling the bottle cap with warm water and adding a single grain of turquoise dishwashing detergent. Marvin sank into the bubbles and floated in the pool to his heart's content, until he was shiny and clean again.

THE BIRTHDAY PARTY

The next day was Saturday, James's birthday. There was to be a party, a large one, and the Pompadays' dining room was festooned with streamers and balloons. As Marvin and his parents foraged for breakfast under the kitchen table, they listened to the plans.

"I don't want those boys eating in the living room," Mrs. Pompaday told James. "Make sure they stay at the table when it's time for the cake."

"But, Mom," James said. "I can't tell them what to do. They're not even my friends."

William banged deafeningly on his highchair tray with a spoon and crowed at

James. "Ya ya! Ya ya!" From what Marvin could tell, this was the word for James in William's very limited but forceful language.

"What a big boy you are!" Mrs. Pompaday crooned, wiping the baby's face with a washcloth. She turned to James. "What do you mean they're not your friends? Why, the Fentons live right upstairs. You see Max every day."

James sighed.

"They're very important clients of mine, the Fentons. I've gotten several referrals from them, and you know, that's the heart of my business. Word of mouth." Below the table, Mama and Papa looked at each other and rolled their eyes. "So I hope you'll treat Max nicely, dear," Mrs. Pompaday continued.

Mama shook her head, whispering, "Clients! Will he have a single one of his own friends at the party?" she asked.

"Of course not," Papa replied.

Marvin had seen enough of Mrs. Pompaday's parties to know that his parents were right. Whatever the occasion, the guest list was always a loose assemblage of people she worked with or wanted to work with, and for the entire party Mrs. Pompaday would float fawningly from one person to the next, confiding self-important tips about the Manhattan real estate market.

Mrs. Pompaday plucked William from the high chair and said encouragingly, "We're having a magician, remember? You know how you love magic, James."

James hesitated. "Mom . . . don't you think that's the kind of thing people have at a little kid's party?"

"Nonsense, dear. Everyone loves magicians. They're like clowns."

Marvin personally hated clowns, which he had seen in abundance on television because Mr. Pompaday had an odd fascination with the circus. Clowns struck Marvin as scary and untrustworthy, with their painted faces and exaggerated expressions, always trying to get strangers to laugh.

The beetles had learned most of what they

knew about the outside world from the Pompadays' endless stream of television shows. Mrs. Pompaday's favorites were hospital dramas or soap operas, while Mr. Pompaday preferred long documentaries on obscure topics. James liked cartoons, which Marvin found colorful and quite satisfying, especially when they featured a heroic or particularly energetic insect. The best thing about television in the Pompaday household was that the Pompadays tended to snack while they watched their shows, so the beetles could count on a veritable smorgasbord of popcorn kernels, raisins, and potato-chip crumbs at the end of the evening.

Marvin watched James, who was jiggling a sneaker. "Mom," James said, "do you think Dad will come?"

"I don't know, James. He said he'd try. But it's going to be a wonderful party, you'll see!" Mrs. Pompaday swept over and kissed the top of his head. "Stop moping. It's your birthday! Come help me with the goody bags."

James's father was an artist, the maker of large abstract paintings, one of which, a mostly blue canvas called *Horse,* hung above the couch in the living room. It was a constant source of tension between Mrs. Pompaday and her second husband.

"I don't see why I have to look at that every night," Mr. Pompaday would complain. "It doesn't look anything like a horse. It doesn't even look like an animal. James could have painted that."

Mrs. Pompaday's answer was always the same. "Oh, stop. It goes with the rug. Do you know how hard it is to match an Oriental?"

Marvin secretly admired the painting very much. He sometimes climbed all the way up the brass floor lamp for a better view of the bold blue streak at its center. While the painting didn't look like a horse, it *felt* like a horse: fast and graceful and free.

"What can we give James for his birthday?" he asked his parents, as they lugged two cereal flakes and a crumb of buttered toast back to the cupboard. "It has to be something *great*."

"Look in the treasure box," Mama said. "I'm sure you'll find the perfect thing."

The treasure box was an open velvet earring case that had been very difficult indeed to push and tug into the beetles' home. It was filled with the kinds of tiny things humans tended to drop or misplace, items that rolled under furniture or got caught in the cracks between floorboards — or, as William became more dextrous, the things he enjoyed sticking through the grates of the heating vents. Right now, the treasure box contained a few paper clips, two coins, a button, the gold clasp from a necklace, the slender silver bar that once held a watch strap in place, a small eraser, a pen cap, and, the most prized object of all, a single pearl earring.

The beetles happened to know that the pearl earring, found in the wreckage of the Pompadays' annual holiday party, belonged to a favorite client of Mrs. Pompaday's, who had called the next day in a tizzy over its loss. Generally, Mama felt strongly that particularly valuable items should be returned to their human owners (which just meant that the beetles carried them to some obvious spot in the house and left them in full view, where they would inevitably be discovered and exclaimed over in relief). However, in this case, Mr. and Mrs. Pompaday had been so unpleasant to James in the wake of the party — berating him for a china plate that he'd accidentally dropped when his mother asked him to clear the dishes — that the beetles were not inclined to return the pearl earring.

"I don't think there's anything good for James in the treasure box," Marvin said worriedly. "None of that stuff is his."

"Does he have any electronics in need of repair?" Mama asked. "Clock radio? Boom box? I'm sure Albert would be happy to tinker with something for him."

Uncle Albert had trained as an electrician, a particularly useful skill in the Pompadays' aging apartment. He'd been known to fix the faulty wiring in their thermostat on more than one occasion . . . though he sometimes raised the apartment's heat to insufferable levels in the process. "Tricky business, thermostats," he always said.

"No, I don't think so," Marvin answered. "I haven't heard him complain about anything." Although, he realized, James wasn't really the type to complain.

"What about one of the coins in the treasure box?" Papa suggested. "I think there's a buffalo nickel."

Marvin thought about that. Would James even notice that it was a special nickel? Probably. James was the type to notice things. "Maybe," he said. "If we can't find anything better."

The party was a boisterous disaster. Mr. Pompaday was dispatched to the park with William, while eleven energetic boys, none of whom paid any particular attention to James, raced through the apartment. They

34

dumped elaborately wrapped presents on the sideboard, then stampeded from room to room, whooping loudly. They broke a knob off the stereo. They spilled soda on the dining-room rug. They locked a small, nervous boy named Simon in James's closet without anyone realizing he was missing. When the magician arrived, they gleefully tormented him, yelling out spoilers — "It's in his other hand! I saw it!" — as he performed his tricks. One boy dug around in the leather bag of props when the magician wasn't watching and triumphantly brandished a set of handcuffs. "Let's play jail!"

Marvin watched the whole affair from a safe vantage point behind the skirt of the living-room couch. Sneakers pounded past him, squeaking on the wood floors. He kept warily out of sight, heeding Mama's warning: "Whatever you do, darling, don't let them see you. These are the kinds of boys who'd pull the legs off a beetle just for the fun of it." It was an oft-repeated adage among the beetles that human parties were no place for their kind. Marvin remembered all too clearly the fate of his grandfather, who'd been crushed by a stiletto heel while pursuing a bacon bit during the Pompadays' meet-the-neighbors party.

From behind the skirting, Marvin could

see James sitting quietly on the sideline. Mrs. Pompaday kept prodding him in exasperation:

"James! Don't just sit there like that. Show the boys your new computer."

"James, thank Henry for this lovely red sweater. It will be perfect for Valentine's Day."

"James, tell Max about the wonderful time we had skating last week. At the Rockefeller Center rink, Max. We love to go there on weekday afternoons, when there aren't so many tourists. We'll bring you with us next time, shall we?"

From a past conversation, Marvin knew that the Pompadays had been to the rink exactly once, that Mrs. Pompaday had dropped James off while she went across the street to Saks to buy a wedding present, and that James, who didn't know how to skate, had spent the hour clinging to the side wall, unsteadily making his way around the circle while more experienced skaters zipped past.

The doorbell rang, and Mrs. Pompaday clapped her hands, smiling brightly. "Oh, look at the time! Your parents are here, boys." She herded them toward the entryway. "Come get your goody bags! James, dear, stand by the door and hand them out."

Marvin, risking exposure, darted along the baseboard to the marble-floored foyer. When Mrs. Pompaday opened the door, however, it wasn't the hoped-for cavalcade of parents, it was Karl Terik, James's father. Mrs. Pompaday stepped back in disappointment. "Oh," she said, "Karl."

The other boys thundered away in indifference. James's whole face lit up. "Dad! You came."

James's father was a big man with longish brown hair and a messy scruff of beard. He had a warm, gentle smile that Marvin liked because it spread across his face so slowly that it had to be real. "Hey, buddy," he said to James. "Of course I came. . . . It's your birthday!" He grabbed James by both shoulders and wrapped him in a hug.

"You can come in for a minute," Mrs. Pompaday said crisply, "but the boys are about to be picked up, and I need James to hand out the goody bags while I speak to their parents."

"Cutting deals?" Karl asked, still smiling.

"No, no," Mrs. Pompaday said dismissively, then added in a lower voice, "but you'll see that Meredith Steinberg's son is here, and they're in the market for a classic six, so it certainly wouldn't hurt for me to say a few words to her."

37

Marvin had often wondered how someone like Karl Terik could ever have been married to Mrs. Pompaday. They seemed profoundly different. He'd overheard James ask his father a similar question once, hesitantly, as if he wasn't quite sure he wanted to hear the answer. Karl had said simply, "Your mother has excellent taste. She always did, from the day I met her. An eye for beauty is a rare thing."

Good taste, to Marvin, didn't seem like much of a foundation for love. Then again, it had turned out not to be.

Karl was ruffling James's hair with one hand. "I brought you something," he said, setting a crumpled plastic shopping bag on the hallway table.

Marvin edged away from the baseboard, trying to see. What was it? What would James want it to be?

James grinned at his father and reached inside. He drew out a small navy blue box, which he opened carefully.

"Oh," he said.

Marvin climbed quickly up one of the slippery polished table legs to have a look. The box contained a squat glass bottle filled with dark liquid.

"It's ink," said Karl.

James said nothing, turning it over in his hand. Marvin could tell he was disappointed.

"It's a pen-and-ink set. For drawing." Karl rustled in the bag and pulled out a flat black case. "Here's the pen. Look, your initials, so everyone will know it's yours." Marvin could see that there were three crisp gold letters on the top. "And I got you a pad of good paper, too," Karl added.

James tilted the bottle of ink, watching the liquid shift inside, catching the light. "Cool," he said. He looked up at his father. "Thanks, Dad. It's really cool."

"Is that permanent ink?" Mrs. Pompaday demanded. "Does it stain?"

"Well, yes. . . . That's what you use for pen-and-ink drawings."

Mrs. Pompaday sighed. "It had better stay in your room, James. On your desk. I don't want ink splattered all over the house." She shook her head. "Really, Karl. That doesn't seem a very appropriate gift for an eleven-year-old."

Karl shifted uncomfortably. "He'll be careful with it, you know that. James is careful with everything."

Mrs. Pompaday snorted.

"It will be fun for him to experiment," Karl said, looping one arm over James's narrow shoulders and pulling him close. "Look at the pen, buddy."

James lifted the pen and unscrewed the cap. Marvin could see that the pen was slim and elegant, with a delicate silver nib.

"Wow," James said, clearly trying to muster some enthusiasm.

"This is how you fill it," Karl said, demonstrating. "Watch the position of your hand while you're drawing, so you don't smear the ink. It'll take a while to get the hang of it."

The doorbell rang again.

"Oh, here they are," Mrs. Pompaday cried. "Boys! James, hurry, the goody bags." She nudged Karl toward the door. "You can show all this to him tomorrow when he's with you," she said. "You'll pick him up at noon?"

"Yeah, or a little after. That okay, James?"

James looked from his father to his mother and nodded quickly. "Sure, Dad."

Mrs. Pompaday pursed her lips, sweeping past him. "Well, I'd like to know what time to expect you. We have plans tomorrow afternoon. If you're going to cancel like last time, you need to at least call! It isn't fair to James, and it certainly isn't fair to me. I have a life too, you know."

"Sorry about that," Karl said sheepishly. "Stuff comes up, that's all."

Mrs. Pompaday swung open the door and smiled broadly. "Julie! We've had the most wonderful time; we didn't even notice it was so late. You're going to have trouble dragging Ryan away! Oh, this is James's father,

41

Karl Terik. Yes, that's right, the artist. He's just leaving."

A PRESENT FOR JAMES

That night, when the house was quiet, Marvin and Elaine sorted through the treasure box. Their parents were playing a game of staples in the other room. Staples was the beetles' modified version of the human game horseshoes, in which two teams threw staples at broken toothpicks stuck in the floor. Because each beetle could throw as many as four staples at once, using his front legs, the air was filled with sharp whizzing objects, and the grown-ups preferred to sequester the children in another part of the house before they began.

"Watch out, Albert!" Marvin heard his mother cry. "We have enough holes in the wall as it is."

Marvin and Elaine peered into the treasure box, looking for the perfect gift for James. "There's the nickel," Marvin said.

"Oooo, a buffalo nickel!" Elaine cried. "He'll like that, don't you think? They're rare. He can sell it and buy something better. That's what I'd do."

Marvin touched the dull surface of the coin. "I guess it's the best thing in here," he said, "but I'd rather give him something to keep."

"Well, maybe he will keep it," Elaine said cheerfully. "Boys like to save the silliest things. Look at you with your tack collection. What will you ever use those for?"

"Those are *weapons*," Marvin protested.

Elaine laughed so hard that she fell off the edge of the box and lay on her back, feet waving in the air. "Oh! Help me! Marvin, turn me over."

But Marvin ignored her. He burrowed under the nickel and used his shell to flip it out of the treasure box. Then he heaved it upright and rolled it through the hole in the wall into the black expanse of the cupboard.

"Marvin!" Elaine called. "Come back!"

The journey through the dark apartment to James's room was an arduous one. Rolling the nickel across the kitchen tile went relatively smoothly, but hoisting it over the doorsills left Marvin exhausted and panting. He had to watch for trouble every step of the way, not just night-roving Pompadays, but the booby traps of forgotten gum or Scotch tape on the floor or, worse yet, a foraging mouse.

When he finally reached James's bedroom, he had to sit for a minute to catch his breath. A streetlamp outside the window cast dim light across the walls, and in the bluish blackness Marvin saw the mountainous silhouette of James, asleep under the blankets. He heard the boy's deep breaths.

Marvin thought about the birthday party. Had it been a good day for James? The boys at the party weren't his friends. The presents had been an uninspired mix of electronic games and designer clothing. Mrs. Pompaday was as fussy and self-centered as always, and even James's father, whom Marvin liked a lot, hadn't come up with a present that seemed to please his son. Marvin glanced down at the worn face of the buffalo nickel. Would the coin make up for everything else? Probably not.

Suddenly, Marvin felt so sad he could hardly stand it. A person's birthday should be a special day, a wonderful day, a day of pure celebration for the luck of being born! And James's birthday had been miserable.

Marvin rolled the nickel to a prominent place in the middle of the floor, away from the edge of the rug where it might be overlooked. James would see it there. He looked around the dark room one last time.

Then he saw the bottle of ink. It was high up on James's desk, and it appeared to be open.

Curious, Marvin crawled across the floor to the desk and quickly climbed to the top. James had spread newspaper over the desk and two or three sheets of the art paper his father had given him. On one page he'd made some experimental scribbles and had written his name. The pen, neatly capped, rested at the edge of the paper, but the bottle of ink stood open, glinting in the weak light.

Without really thinking about what he was doing, Marvin crawled to the cap of the bottle and dipped his two front legs in the ink that had pooled inside. On his clean hind legs, he backed over to an unused sheet of paper. He looked out the window at the nightscape of the street: the brownstone opposite with its rows of darkened windows, the snow-dusted rooftop, the streetlamp, the naked, spidery branches of a single tree.

Gently, delicately, and with immense concentration, Marvin lowered his front legs and began to draw.

The ink flowed smoothly off his legs across the page. Though he'd never done anything like this before, it seemed completely natural, even unstoppable. He kept glancing up, tracing the details of the scene with his eyes, then transferring them onto the paper. It was as if his legs had been waiting all their lives for this ink, this page, this lamp-lit window view. There was no way to describe the feeling. It thrilled Marvin to his very core.

He drew and drew, losing all sense of time. He moved back and forth between the ink cap and the paper, dipping his front legs gently in the puddle of black ink, always careful not to smear his previous work. He watched the picture take shape before his eyes. It was a complicated thatching of lines and whirls that looked like an abstract design up close, as Marvin leaned over it. But as he backed away, it transformed into a meticulous portrait of the cityscape: a tiny, detailed replica of the winter scene outside the window.

And then the light changed. The sky turned from black to dark blue to gray, the streetlamp shut off, and James's room was filled with the noise of the city waking. A garbage truck groaned and banged as it passed on the street below. James stirred beneath his bedcovers. Marvin, desperate to finish his picture before the boy awakened, hurried between the page and the ink cap, which was almost out of ink. At last he stopped, surveying his miniature scene.

It was finished.

It was perfect.

It was breathtaking.

Marvin's heart swelled. He felt that he had never done anything so fine or important in his entire life. He wiped his ink-soaked forelegs on the newspaper and scurried behind the desk lamp, bursting with pride, in a fever of anticipation, just as James threw off his blankets.

James stumbled out of bed and stood in the center of the bedroom, rubbing his face. He looked around groggily, then straightened, his eyes lighting on the floor.

"Hey," he said softly. He padded over to the nickel and crouched, picking it up.

Good for James, thought Marvin. Of course there was no reason to worry that he'd overlook it.

James turned the coin over in his palm and smiled. "Huh," he said, walking toward his desk. "I wonder where this came from."

Marvin stiffened and retreated farther behind the desk lamp.

James gasped.

Marvin watched James's pale face, his eyes huge as he stared at the drawing. He quickly looked behind him, as if the room might hold some clue that would explain what he saw on his desk.

Then slowly, brows furrowed, James pulled out the chair and sat down. He leaned over the picture. "Wow," he said. "Wow!"

Marvin straightened with pride.

James kept examining the drawing, then the scene through the window, whispering to himself. "It's exactly like what's outside! It's like a teeny-tiny picture of the street! This is amazing."

Marvin crept around the base of the lamp so he could hear the boy better.

"But . . . how?" James picked up the pen and uncapped it, squinting. He lifted the bottle of ink and frowned, screwing the ink cap back on. "Who did this?" he asked, staring again at the picture.

And then, without planning to — without meaning to, without ever thinking for a moment of the consequences — Marvin found himself crawling out into the open, across the vast desktop, directly in front of James. He stopped at the edge of the picture and waited, unable to breathe.

James stared at him.

After a long, interminable silence, during which Marvin almost dashed to the grooved safety of the wainscoting behind the desk, James spoke.

"It was you, wasn't it?" he said.

Marvin waited.

"But how?"

Marvin hesitated. He crawled over to the bottle of ink.

James reached across the desk, and Marvin cringed as enormous pinkish fingers swept tremblingly close to his shell. But the boy avoided him, carefully lifting the bottle and shaking it. He unscrewed the cap and set it down next to Marvin.

"Show me," he whispered.

Marvin dipped his two front legs in the ink cap and walked across the page to his picture. Unwilling to change the details of the image, he merely traced the line that framed it, then stepped back.

"With your legs? Like that? Dipping them

in the ink?" A wide grin full of wonderment and delight spread across James's face. "You really did that! A bug! That's the most incredible thing I ever, ever, ever saw in my whole entire life!"

Marvin beamed up at him.

"And with my birthday present too! You couldn't have done it without my birthday present." His voice rose excitedly as he leaned closer to Marvin, his warm breath almost blasting Marvin over.

"It's like we're a team. And you know what? I didn't even want this birthday present before. I thought, 'What am I going to do with this? I'm not like my dad. I don't even know how to draw.' But now, it's the best gift I ever got. This birthday is the best one ever!"

Marvin smiled happily. He realized that James could not for one minute see his expression, but he suspected somehow that the boy knew anyway.

Just then, they heard a noise in the hallway and Mrs. Pompaday's voice: "James, what are you doing in there? Who are you talking to?"

Marvin dove for cover, squeezing under James's china piggy bank at the exact moment that Mrs. Pompaday swept into the room.

"It's remarkable!"

James leapt away from the desk. "Hi, Mom," he said nervously. "I'm, um, just getting ready for church."

"Well, you need to hurry, dear." His mother leaned over to kiss James on the cheek, balancing William on her hip. The baby flung himself forward, burbling excitedly. "Ya YA! Ya ya!"

Mrs. Pompaday tried to restrain him. "Yes, William, that's JAMES. Can you say 'Ja-Ja-Ja-James'?" When the baby grabbed a fistful of her jacket, she chided, "Don't muss Mommy's nice blazer," then redirected her attention to her older son. "We don't want to be late, James. Everyone in this house is so slow in the mornings! Sometimes I think I'm the only one who cares about looking presentable and being on time." She checked her hair in James's mirror, patting it approvingly. "Who were you talking to?"

"Nobody," James said. "Just myself."

"Well, try not to do that. It's not normal. Oh, I don't want to see that ink bottle uncapped, James! It'll get knocked over. You promised to be —"

James hurriedly shuffled the pages on the desk, trying to hide Marvin's drawing. But he wasn't fast enough. Mrs. Pompaday marched across the room and lifted the paper.

"What's this?"

James hesitated. He looked in the direction of the piggy bank, where Marvin crouched out of sight. "Nothing. Just . . . just a picture."

"Yes, I can see that." Mrs. Pompaday turned the page in her hand, studying it. "Where did you get it?"

Don't tell her, Marvin thought. *Please don't tell her.*

He had a sudden understanding of how grave a risk he'd taken: drawing the picture, showing himself to James, taking credit for the artwork. Not only was he personally in danger if Mrs. Pompaday realized a beetle

had done the drawing, but his whole family would be in jeopardy as soon as she discovered there were beetles in the house . . . artistically talented ones or not. She wasn't a woman with a tolerance for bugs.

Mrs. Pompaday continued to stare at the picture. "Did it come with the ink set, as an example?" she asked. She turned slowly toward the window, still holding the page. "Oh . . . why . . . oh, my goodness! James! Did you draw this? Why, it's . . . I can't believe it. It's remarkable!"

Marvin watched James's face from his viewpoint under the piggy bank. He saw so many feelings chase across it — worry, then surprise, then a flash of pure joy as his mother exclaimed over the drawing.

"James, I had no idea you could draw like this." William lunged for the paper and Mrs.

Pompaday raised it out of his reach. "No, William, mustn't touch." She held it at arm's length, scrutinizing it. "I don't understand why your art teacher at school hasn't spoken to me. You've a fantastic talent, dear!"

Marvin saw James open his mouth to protest, then weakly close it. His mother continued to gush. "This is — well, it's astounding, that's what it is. Such cunning detail. I must show it to Bob."

She called repeatedly for Mr. Pompaday, who eventually appeared in the doorway, tightening his tie. "Yes? What's the fuss?"

"Bob, look at this. Look at the wonderful picture our James has made."

Mr. Pompaday considered the drawing and harrumphed. "James couldn't have drawn that. It looks like some kind of museum reproduction, like one of those old engravings."

"I know, I know," Mrs. Pompaday agreed. "That's what I thought myself. But, look, it's the scene outside James's window! He drew it with his new pen-and-ink set."

Mr. Pompaday took the paper and walked to the window. He surveyed the street and looked back at the picture. "Huh," he said. "So it is." He squinted irritably at James. "Where'd you get the art set?"

"From my dad," James said, looking down. "For my birthday."

"That's right, Karl stopped by yesterday," Mrs. Pompaday added in a rush. "Dropped off a pen-and-ink set for James. I didn't think much of the idea, myself. An eleven-year-old boy using permanent ink? But look what James made! Honestly, I can hardly believe it. I never imagined he had this kind of gift!"

Marvin winced.

Mrs. Pompaday went on, "I suppose, with his father being an artist, I did suspect that James might have some sort of aptitude in that area, but really —"

Mr. Pompaday frowned. "Karl! This is much better than that hogwash Karl paints. This actually looks like something."

"I know. Isn't it splendid? I can't wait to show it to the Mortons. They're always purchasing those fancy little sketches at Sotheby's for outrageous sums. Wait till they see what my own child has drawn." Mrs. Pompaday squeezed James's shoulder, and William reached for a fistful of his hair. James smiled uncertainly, batting William's hand away.

"Well, um, should I get ready for church?" he asked.

"Look at the time!" Mr. Pompaday snapped. "Yes, hurry up, James. We have to leave in twenty minutes." He grabbed William from his wife and stomped into the hall.

Mrs. Pompaday started to follow him, the drawing in her hand. But James touched

58

her sleeve. "Mom, could I keep the picture here? With my ink set?"

"Oh." Mrs. Pompaday hesitated. "Yes, of course. I'd like to show it to a few people, that's all. It really is so lovely." She placed it regretfully on the desk. "You'll be careful, won't you, James? Not to spill anything on it? Perhaps you could work on another one this afternoon."

James shot an awkward glance at Marvin. "I don't know, Mom . . . maybe. But Dad's coming, remember? And it would take me a while."

"Oh, I can imagine it would! I don't know when you found time for it yesterday, with the party and everything else." She smiled at him again. "I can't believe you were able to draw this, James. And think: If you hadn't gotten that ink set, we might never have discovered this fabulous talent of yours!"

As she clicked out of the room, something about her approving gaze reminded Marvin of his own mother, who would be frantic with worry back at home. He'd been gone all night. His parents would have no idea what had happened to him. With the coast clear, he sped across the desktop and down the wooden leg to the floor.

"Wait!" James cried. "Where are you going?"

But Marvin dashed away, feeling comfortingly certain that his new friend wouldn't try to stop him.

A New Kind of Trouble

When Marvin finally crawled through the cupboard wall into the family's living room, he was greeted by a dozen of his relatives in an anxious huddle. Their faces lit with relief when they saw him. Only cousin Elaine seemed somewhat let down.

His mother rushed to him, gathering him in her many legs. "Marvin! Oh, darling, where were you? You gave us such a fright!"

"What happened, son?" Papa pressed. "Elaine said you'd gone to deliver the nickel, but when Albert and I went looking for you, we couldn't find you anywhere."

"We thought something terrible had happened to you," Elaine added, her voice grave. "Why, it could have been anything. You might have caught a leg in one of the floorboards, or the nickel could have fallen on top of you, or you might have been crushed underfoot by one of the Pompadays making a midnight trip to the bath —"

"That's enough, Elaine," Uncle Albert said severely.

But Marvin's grandmother was not so easily quieted. "Marvin, Marvin! Have you forgotten about Uncle George?" she cried, hugging him close. "Is life so cheap?"

Marvin sighed. Of course he hadn't forgotten about Uncle George. Who could forget about Uncle George, whose fate was the subject of frequent cautionary lectures by the adults in the family? The lead tuba player in the neighborhood band, Uncle George had ventured out one night with the bass guitarist to retrieve a piece of dry macaroni (his preferred instrument) from beneath the stove. They were intercepted by a particularly bold and hungry mouse. The guitarist escaped, but Uncle George was not so lucky.

"I'm sorry," Marvin said. "I didn't mean for anyone to worry. I was in James's room, up on his desk. That's why you didn't see me, Papa."

"But, darling, whatever were you doing

there?" Mama asked anxiously. "James isn't allowed to eat in his room, you know that. There wouldn't have been any food."

"No, I wasn't looking for food." Marvin hesitated, scanning the ring of puzzled faces. Even his cousin Billy, the wild one who'd lost a leg surfing in the garbage disposal, had never gone missing for an entire night. In the beetles' world, that inevitably spelled doom. There were too many things that could go wrong.

"Then what, Marvin?" Papa asked. "What were you doing?"

"I —" Marvin didn't know how to explain it. The wonder of the drawing seemed too new to him, too fragile to share with his family. He took a deep breath. "I wanted to do something for James, because his birthday party was so awful. You know how he got that ink set from his dad? Well, it was on the desk, with the cap off."

"Don't tell me you fell in!" Mama gasped.

"No! No, Mama."

The family waited.

"I dipped my front legs in the ink and drew a picture for him."

The room fell silent. Marvin looked from his mother to his father.

"A *picture?*" Papa asked. "What kind of picture?"

"The scene outside his window," Marvin mumbled, studying the floor. "The building across the street, with the tree and the streetlamp. Just a tiny picture of it."

"But, Marvin," Mama said softly. "You could have been caught. And now . . . the picture . . . well, what will James think? Is it even big enough for him to see it? And if it is, who will he think drew such a thing? He's too old to believe in fairies."

Marvin paused. "He knows I did it."

"WHAT?" The cry came in unison from the assembled relatives, their faces frozen in horror.

Marvin hurriedly explained what had happened. "But James won't tell anyone. I know he won't. He wouldn't do anything to get me in trouble."

Mama shook her head. "Marvin, I know you like James — we all do — but he's a HUMAN. He has no loyalty to our kind. Humans can't be trusted."

Papa turned to Uncle Albert. "We'll have to get the drawing. That's the only answer."

"No, Papa, you can't!" Marvin cried. "It was a present for James. I made it for him. And Mr. and Mrs. Pompaday have seen it now. They think he was the one who drew it. You should have seen how happy that made him! You can't just take it away."

"Marvin," his father said sternly. "I don't think you understand the gravity of this situation."

His grandmother nodded. "I know you meant well, dear boy, but that drawing endangers all of us."

Marvin turned desperately to his mother, but her response was firm. "James can't keep it, darling, especially now that he knows you're responsible."

There was a murmur of assent from the relatives.

"You'll have to get it back."

"Go now, while they're at church."

"Paper's heavy. You'll need a few extra legs."

Marvin looked around the room in utter dejection.

"Okay," he said finally.

Miserably, he led a small posse of beetles — consisting of his parents, Uncle Albert, Uncle Ted, and Elaine — out of the cupboard and through the quiet apartment in the direction of James's room.

When the six beetles finally reached the desktop, the picture was right where James had left it, resting at an angle atop the scattered sheets of newspaper. Marvin felt his heart leap wildly at the sight of it. His parents stopped dead in their tracks.

"Marvin," Mama said, her voice hushed.

Papa's jaw dropped. "Son, you *made* this?"

Elaine crawled eagerly across the paper, gushing praise. "Marvin, it's beautiful! The lines are so little and neat. It looks exactly like what's outside! And you drew it in the dark too. I'd like to see a human try that. They can't see for beans at night."

"It's stunning, my boy," Uncle Albert agreed. "There's no other word for it."

Uncle Ted clapped Mama on the back. "Marvin's an artist! We've got a real artist in the family! Do you remember Jeannie's murals, the ones she made with toothpaste? She wasn't nearly this good."

Marvin glowed with pride.

Mama stroked his shell. "It's a marvelous

picture, darling. Just marvelous . . . so beautiful and true. I can't imagine how you did it. No wonder James was pleased. What a gift!"

Papa studied the drawing regretfully. "And what a shame we have to take it away."

Just then they heard the front door unlatch

and a commotion in the foyer, punctuated by William's trademark bellow.

"Oh! The Pompadays are home from church!" Mama cried. "Quick, try to lift it."

The beetles surrounded the paper, one at each end, two on the long sides, and wedged their shells under the edges. They could hear James's sneakered feet thudding down the hall.

"There's no time," Papa hissed. "We can't do it."

"Hurry, everyone, under the piggy bank and down the wall," Uncle Ted ordered.

"What — are we just going to leave Marvin's picture?" Elaine protested. "After all this, we're not taking it with us?"

"Elaine, hush," Uncle Albert scolded. "James will be here in one second."

The beetles dashed for cover just as James came racing into the room. They clustered for a moment beneath the piggy bank, then Uncle Ted climbed from the desk to the grooved wainscoting and started down the wall, leading the way.

Marvin hung back in the shadow of the piggy bank. "Papa," he whispered, "can I stay for a little while? I want to see what he'll do with the drawing."

His father hesitated, poised between the wooden edge of the desk and the wall. "I don't think that's a good idea, son."

"But he might move it, and that way I'll know where it is."

Papa frowned, considering. "I suppose that would be helpful." His eyes followed the retreating line of beetles, already halfway down the wall. "All right," he decided. "But you need to keep yourself hidden this time, Marvin. Do you understand? And we'll expect you home by dinner."

"Oh, I will be, Papa!" Marvin promised. "That's hours and hours away."

"IT COULD BE A DÜRER."

Cautiously, Marvin crawled over to his preferred spying place behind the desk lamp, watching James the whole time. James was leaning over the drawing, studying it, his face transfixed in a smile. Suddenly, he looked up. He peered around the top of the desk.

"Hey, little guy," he said softly.

Marvin stiffened. He'd thought he was well hidden behind the lamp's brass base, but James's voice suggested otherwise. Remembering Papa's warning, he flattened himself and slid partway under the lamp.

James kept talking, his voice calm. "Little guy, that's what I'll call you . . . because

70

you are a really little guy." He hesitated. "Unless you're a girl."

WHAT? Marvin recoiled in alarm, despite his determination to keep still.

"Don't be scared. I won't hurt you," James said. He continued to study Marvin. "I don't think you're a girl. I think you're a boy, like me."

Marvin felt a flicker of relief, but stayed frozen at the edge of the lamp.

"You probably can't even understand me, huh? That's okay. My dad is coming in a few minutes. I can't wait to show him your picture! It's the most amazing thing."

Marvin watched James lean his elbows on the desk, settling his face in his hands. "But everyone thinks I did it. That's the only problem. And I don't know how to tell them."

James's serious gray eyes tracked over to the lamp and stayed there. Marvin cringed.

"They'll never believe you did it, anyway. So what's the point of telling them?"

No point, Marvin wanted to say. *Don't bother, especially since the drawing won't even be here tomorrow. Best to forget all this.* He gazed at the tiny picture mournfully.

From the hall they heard a loud thump on the door, and Mrs. Pompaday's muted greeting. A minute later, Karl Terik and

71

Mrs. Pompaday appeared in the doorway.

"James! James, show your father your drawing. Look at this, Karl. You'll be shocked, I tell you. Look how tiny and elegant it is. Oh, I can't wait to show it to the Mortons. And Sandra Ortiz, at the gallery."

Karl grinned at James and strode over to the desk, wearing a patient expression, as if preparing to compliment the picture no matter what he really thought. But when he saw Marvin's drawing, his eyes widened. He rubbed his beard, staring at it.

"May I?" he asked James, reaching for the paper.

James blushed. "Sure, Dad."

Marvin inched forward to watch Karl's reaction.

"James," his father said slowly.

"What did I tell you?" Mrs. Pompaday clapped her hands. "Isn't it wonderful?"

Karl walked to the window, lifting the drawing to the light. "How did you do this?"

James swallowed. "I just did it. You know, copied what was outside."

His father brought the page close to his face, scrutinizing it, then held it at arm's length. "The lines are so delicate. And steady. I wouldn't have thought you could make a line this thin with the pen I gave you."

James didn't say anything.

Karl shook his head. "It looks . . . well, it's ridiculous to say it, but it could be a Dürer."

Marvin and James both stared at him, not understanding. Karl was still lost in thought, tilting the drawing at different angles. "I mean it. It's that good."

Mrs. Pompaday glowed. "Oh, yes! Exactly. A Dürer."

"What's that?" James asked. "What's a dürer?"

"Albrecht Dürer," Karl explained. "The German Renaissance artist. Painter, engraver, did lots of pen-and-ink drawings, even a few miniatures like this, a long, long time ago. The detail in this is unbelievable, James. I can't get over it."

James smiled joyfully at his parents. Marvin smiled joyfully at James.

"How long did it take you?" his father continued.

James squinted in the direction of the desk lamp and bit his lip. "Um, I don't know, I wasn't paying attention," he said. "But it took a while."

"I bet so," his father said, whistling under his breath. He dropped his hand to James's back and rubbed the boy's thin neck, his

73

voice rising in excitement. "You know what we'll do, buddy? We'll go to the Met this afternoon! There's a drawing exhibit that just opened, works by the Old Masters — Dürer, Bellini, Titian, Michelangelo. You have to see it. Here, we'll take your drawing with us."

Marvin almost toppled out into the open. *No!* he wanted to cry. *Stop him, James!*

But Karl grabbed a math textbook from the desk and carefully slipped the drawing inside the cover. "I want you to see firsthand how good this is," he told James.

"Really?" James asked. "You think it's as good as the pictures by those famous guys?"

"I do! I really do, James." His father ruffled his hair.

Mrs. Pompaday didn't look pleased. "I don't think you should take that drawing anywhere," she said. "What if something happens to it? I haven't even had a chance to show my friends."

Karl laughed. "Nothing will happen to it," he said, tucking the math book securely under one arm. "I'll guard it with my life. This is really something!"

Now what? Marvin raced back and forth behind the base of the lamp, not knowing what to do. What if they took the drawing away for good?

James and his parents were heading through the door when Marvin saw James hesitate. "Oops, my jacket," he said to his father. He came back into the room, grabbing it from his closet, then paused by the desk, crouching near Marvin and shielding him from his parents' view.

"Come with us," he whispered. "To see the drawings. Don't you want to?" He rested one big pale finger on the desktop next to Marvin, his eyes urgent. "Come on, I'll take care of you. We'll be back soon."

Marvin was unable to think of anything but the drawing, which was now gone, out of the room, headed to the Metropolitan Museum of Art. He dithered for one tor-

mented moment, then scrambled on top of James's warm, fleshy finger.

"Here, I'll put you someplace safe," James whispered. He gently deposited Marvin in the pocket of his jacket. Frightened but thrilled, Marvin clung to the lip of the nylon fabric, peering out at the swiftly passing world from an unaccustomed height.

THE TEMPLE OF ART

In his entire life, Marvin had never been outside the Pompadays' apartment. To be fair, he had crawled onto James's window ledge once or twice. On an unexpectedly warm day in December, the Pompadays' cleaning woman had opened a few windows to let the mild air swirl through the winter-stale rooms, and Marvin had climbed eagerly onto the sill, scanning the distant sky above and the narrow, bustling street below. For all the information he'd gleaned from the Pompadays' television shows, the world beyond the apartment still seemed vast and unknowable.

Marvin couldn't believe that here he was,

tucked in James's jacket, venturing out into the city. He held on to the nylon pocket with only his head protruding. The crisp February chill stung his shell, and the sidewalk rocked along below at an astonishing speed. Pedestrians loomed in front of him and quickly passed. Cars roared by, then squealed to a stop, horns blaring. Everything seemed too large, too loud, too strange. Marvin knew there must be beetles living out here too. He knew his own family had relations in Gramercy Park. He couldn't help but wonder how they managed in a world that changed so quickly every minute. The city was full of danger and life. Marvin felt dizzy with excitement.

As he jostled along in James's pocket, he remembered the story of Aunt Cecile, the traveler of the family, known for her wanderlust. One summer day, she'd absconded from the kitchen with a used tea bag, opened one end to meticulously empty the contents of the pouch, and then used it as a parachute to leap from the living-room window, holding fast to the string.

The beetles had watched her drift gamely to earth. A tiny floating speck, she disappeared when she reached the sidewalk and was never seen again. Marvin thought of her out here somewhere in the huge, hurrying world. Did she regret her boldness? Or had it been the first essential step, opening her life to new, unprecedented adventures?

"Is that it?" James asked, pointing to the enormous grayish white edifice that rose before them.

"Yep, that's the Met," his father told him. "You've been here before, remember? Though I mostly take you to the Museum of Modern Art."

Marvin could see large colorful banners with writing on them hanging high across the front of the building. He had no idea what they said. As easy as it was to understand human speech, and even to eventually figure out the concept of human time, it had proven nearly impossible for the beetles to decode their writing. A written language was something the beetles had no use for among themselves. But Marvin now realized just how helpful it could be. Why, if he knew how to write in James's language, just imagine all the interesting, important things he could tell him!

They climbed the long sweep of stone steps two at a time, with James cupping one hand protectively over his pocket. Soon they were in the cavernous main hall of the

building. Marvin peered around at the crowds of people in their dark winter coats, the large, elegant vases of flowers, and the wide stairs leading to the second floor.

"This way," Karl called, leading them up the central staircase with long strides. Two vaulted hallways stretched on either side, with glass cases that held colorful displays of porcelain bowls and platters. Soft yellow light shrouded the open space.

"I remember this place now," James said. "It kind of feels like a church."

His father smiled. "Well, it kind of *is* a church . . . a temple of art."

Marvin glimpsed marble statues and gilt-framed paintings. Moments later, they walked into a large room, its walls lined with drawings.

"Wow." James stared. "Look at all this stuff."

His father took his hand and pulled him along. "I think the Dürer drawings are in the third room."

Marvin was too far from the walls and too jostled by his jacket perch to see well, but he could make out a blur of sketches, mostly portraits and figures, sometimes a land-scape. The colors were muted: blacks, grays, browns, a faint wash of red. As soon as James stopped walking, Marvin tried to climb farther out of his pocket to get a better view. James kept sneaking small, worried glances in his direction.

"Here!" his father said finally. "Look at that, will you? Do you see what I mean?"

They came to a stop. By now, Marvin had four legs outside the pocket flap and was balancing precariously on its edge, hoping for a better look. As he teetered there in frustration, James's finger appeared along-side him. He hesitated, then climbed aboard. James raised his hand to his shoul-der, where Marvin quickly disembarked and hid beneath the edge of James's collar.

"Wow!" said James again.

The drawing hanging in front of them was a small, precise image of a courtyard. The lines were impossibly thin and exact; from the casements of the windows to the stones in the square, meticulously contoured. The slate rooftops had edges as sharp as cut glass.

Marvin stared at it. He could almost see the hand of the artist executing each line. The longer he stared, the more he could feel the drawing come into being.

Karl looked around at the other museum-goers, who obliviously walked past them. He set the math book on the floor and carefully removed Marvin's drawing from inside the cover, holding it up and turning to James. "Do you see? Your technique is so similar to Dürer's."

James nodded, speechless.

Slowly they moved along the wall of drawings, stopping to study each one. There were other small landscapes, pictures of an old woman and a girl, a pen-and-ink drawing of a rabbit. They were almost photographic in their details, yet startlingly distinct. The faces looked like real people, Marvin thought, with the ruggedness of noses and chins, expressions full of feeling. Near the end of the wall, James stopped.

"Look at this one, Dad. It's so little.

What's it supposed to be?"

Marvin crept out from under James's collar. The drawing was a tiny framed miniature of a gowned woman kneeling, with her arms around an animal. A lion. She had waves of hair that cascaded down her back, and the lion's mane flowed in similar waves over its massive shoulders.

Karl read the plaque. "It says it's one of

the four cardinal virtues: Fortitude. Do you know what that means?"

"No," said James.

"Courage. Strength."

"Is she trying to catch the lion?"

"Well, sort of wrestling with it, I think. Look at the detail, though. Look at the folds of her dress and the lion's claws. Dürer's hand is so precise. That's what made me think of your drawing, James." Karl squeezed James's shoulder.

I could do that, thought Marvin. He was riveted.

"Karl?"

They all turned at the voice. Emerging from the loose clusters of people in the gallery was one rumpled-looking older man, walking directly toward them and smiling warmly. "I thought that was you."

The Woman and the Lion

"Denny! Hey! How are you?" Karl grinned broadly, thrusting out his hand. "James, this is Dennis MacGuffin, an old friend from my Pratt days. Remember? The art college? Denny, my son, James."

Denny crouched slightly, winking at James. "Not so old, eh, James? It's nice to meet you. I'm always delighted to see young people at an exhibit like this."

"What are you doing here, Denny? I thought you were out west somewhere. . . . California, wasn't it?"

Denny nodded. "Yes, that's right. I'm at the Getty now. Curator of Drawings. The Dürer and this Bellini over here are ours."

He gestured to a similar picture of a woman and a lion, hanging next to the one they were staring at. It was the same size, but Marvin thought it seemed less delicate, the pen strokes thicker.

Denny continued, "We've got a number of items on loan for this exhibit, and I've been helping Ms. Balcony with the arrangements." He beckoned to a woman who was skirting the crowds and walking in their direction, her gaze darting over the drawings.

Marvin edged out from underneath James's collar. She was slim and tidy-looking, her blouse tucked in, her honey-colored hair drawn back in a neat bun. Black rectangular glasses sat firmly on her small nose. He saw that she was very pretty, but she had the unself-conscious manner of someone who was totally oblivious to that fact — which only made her seem prettier. Marvin liked her instantly.

"Christina," Denny called to her. "Come meet my friends Karl Terik and his son, James. You may have heard of Karl's work. He shows at Ernst Auger's gallery. In addition to being one of my favorite people, he's an excellent artist."

Christina Balcony approached them, smiling. "Terik? No, I'm afraid not."

"My *Freedom* series was at the Steinholm last fall. Large abstracts?" Marvin thought Karl sounded embarrassed, but hopeful.

"No, doesn't ring a bell."

"Or maybe you saw some of my work at the Whitney Biennial?"

Christina shook her head. "But anything less than four hundred years old is quite beyond my area of expertise."

"Expertise or interest?" Karl asked, and Marvin was surprised to hear a note of irritation in his voice.

"Well, both, I suppose," she said, laughing. "I'm sorry. Please don't take my ignorance as any sort of verdict on your work.

I'm stuck in the late 1400s . . . Germany, Italy, Holland."

Stuck in the late 1400s. The time of these drawings. Marvin couldn't even imagine how long ago that was. Impossibly ancient, in beetle terms.

Christina took Karl's extended hand and gave James a wide smile. "Do you like these?"

James nodded shyly.

"We do," Karl said. "Very much. Especially the Dürers."

"Yes, they're lovely. He's our favorite, isn't he, Denny? Whenever one of his comes up for sale, we are always fighting over it. Extraordinary attention to detail, and a flawless touch . . . you can really see it here, compared to the Bellini." She turned to James. "Same image, different artist. Which do you like better?"

James looked up at her. "That one," he almost whispered, pointing to the Dürer. *Me too,* thought Marvin. The Bellini was prettier in its way, but Marvin preferred the crisp, certain lines of the Dürer.

"Why?" Christina asked encouragingly. James bit his lip, too shy to answer.

"Giovanni Bellini was a great Italian artist," she said. "Dürer called him 'the best painter of them all.' "

"But he's not nearly as admired as Dürer," Karl pointed out.

"Well, at the time he was. Now he's often overlooked in favor of the big names . . . Michelangelo, Leonardo, Rembrandt." Christina studied the two pictures, smiling faintly. "Dürer went to Venice to learn from Bellini, but look how different the pictures are. The best teachers are like that. They don't teach you how to do things exactly the way they do; they teach you how to be your best self."

She pointed at the Bellini drawing. "This one is gentle, all curves and shadings. The woman almost seems to be playing with the lion."

Marvin could see what she meant. There was nothing particularly threatening about either the girl or the lion, even though the drawing was called *Fortitude.*

"Now look at the Dürer," Christina said. "He tries to capture Bellini's ideal of Italian beauty, but he can't do it. Dürer's girl is a German peasant, a real person. Look at her shoulders. They're as massive as the lion's. It will be a fight to the finish, for sure."

Denny laughed. "And my money's on the girl."

James nodded. Half-hidden beneath his collar, Marvin did too.

"James likes to draw," Karl interjected. "That's why we're here, actually. I gave him a pen-and-ink set for his birthday and, well — look what he came up with." He held out the drawing for them to see, grinning. "I still can't believe he did this."

Christina Balcony stepped forward. Her whole face changed. The pleasant mask of politeness dropped away. She reached for the drawing. "Your son *drew* this?"

Denny peered over her shoulder and sucked in his breath.

Christina crouched next to James, with the drawing between them. "You made this? By yourself?"

James nodded, blushing.

"Were you tracing something?"

"No. It's just — it's just a copy of what's outside my window at home."

Christina straightened and held the drawing at arm's length, next to the works on the wall. "Look how similar it is to our Dürer miniature, the landscape here," she said to Denny. "The execution . . . it's really uncanny."

"I know," said Karl. "That's why we came. I told James this could have been done by a Renaissance master!"

Christina moved along the wall of pictures, still holding the sheet of paper. "The line . . . it has the same fastidiousness. I wouldn't have thought it possible."

Marvin inched forward to hear her words more clearly. *She's talking about my drawing!* he thought with delight. *She's comparing it to these famous pictures!*

Finally, she turned to them, her face flushed.

"James," she said. "Would you come with me? I want to show you something."

The Woman and the Sword

Marvin quickly ducked back under James's collar, worried about being seen. Christina's face was so close, her eyes fixed on James.

James pressed against his father's leg.

"What? Where?" Karl asked.

Christina's gaze returned to the drawing. "It's extraordinary. It's given me an idea."

Denny raised an eyebrow. "Her ideas are dangerous," he said to Karl and James.

"What are you talking about?" Karl turned from one to the other. "We're only here for a couple of hours. I have to get James home by five o'clock."

Christina glanced around the gallery, at the elderly couples and the guided tours murmuring past.

"It won't take long," she said, and Marvin thought her voice had a pleading note. "I'd love it if you could come to my office. I want you to see something."

Karl rested one large hand on James's back. "But we've barely had a chance to look at the exhibit," he said.

"I know," Christina said apologetically. "I won't monopolize your afternoon, I promise. But if you come with me, I can show you some other Dürer drawings. Would you like that, James?"

"I guess," James said, his voice hesitant. He looked up at his father, and Marvin could see Karl's impatience.

"I'm sorry, but I'd really like to take him around the exhibit. That's why we came." He took the drawing from Christina, who released it very reluctantly. "And his mother will be upset if I don't get him home for dinner. Perhaps another time."

Christina pursed her lips. "It won't take long, Mr. Terik."

"Karl."

"Karl. You'll still have time for the exhibit."

Denny, who had been standing nearby with a preoccupied expression, finally intervened. "Karl, if you don't mind, it could be important. I ask you as a favor."

Marvin saw that Karl and Christina were facing each other, equally irritated. Finally, Karl shrugged. "Oh, all right. I don't understand either the urgency or the secrecy, but all right. James?"

James nodded his head, and they followed Christina through the gallery to a plain wood door tucked away in the corner.

"Here?" James asked. "It's like a secret door."

Christina smiled at him. "This is the entrance to the Drawings and Prints Department. Convenient, isn't it?"

"I've got it," Denny said, pulling a small ring of keys from his pocket. He winked at James. "Full access for special friends of the museum. I'm trying to get a lot of use out of these before I have to give them back."

He turned the knob and held the door open for Karl, James, and Christina to enter. Marvin looked around in amazement. The nondescript door opened into a large study lined with bookshelves. There were doors and hallways opening off it, all hidden behind the wall of the gallery.

"How long are you here for, Denny?" Karl asked.

"Just a couple of weeks. Then back to the Getty. I won't be sorry to leave this cold

weather for my California sunshine, I can
tell you that."

Christina Balcony's office was at the end
of a long corridor. It was a large room with
windows overlooking Central Park, and
floor-to-ceiling shelves crammed with books
— probably fat, dusty volumes of art history, Marvin decided. There were a few bat-
tered wooden chairs around a long table.
She indicated to them with one hand while
she retrieved a big book from her desk.
James, his father, and Denny sat down and

waited. Christina balanced the book awkwardly in the crook of her arm and thumbed through the pages to a glossy reproduction of a pen-and-ink drawing.

She set it down in front of James. "It's another Dürer. Like the *Fortitude* drawing. This one is called *Justice.*"

Marvin, still trying to shield himself from sight, could see that the drawing was similar to the drawing of the girl with the lion: the same small size, maybe three or four inches square, same color ink, same impossible level of detail. But this image was of a woman in a long flowing gown with a sword in one hand and a set of scales in the other. Her body was half-turned toward the viewer, and she gazed sadly past him, the scales raised, the sword heavy at her side.

"Is it the same girl as the one with the lion?" James asked.

"No," Christina said. "Look at her face. Dürer's people are always so real, each one distinct. But they share a kind of melancholy."

"What's 'melancholy'?" James asked.

"Sadness," Karl answered, watching Christina.

"Right. A kind of sorrow."

"Why? Why are they sad?" James asked.
Marvin thought they did look a little sad,

but it was more than that. They looked as if they were deep inside themselves, thinking private thoughts.

Christina lifted her shoulders. "Who knows, really? Dürer didn't have a happy life. His marriage was difficult. His wife had a bad temper and cared mostly about money. He threw himself into his art as a way to escape that."

Marvin thought Dürer's wife sounded a little like Mrs. Pompaday.

"But he believed in beauty," Denny added. "He once said, 'What beauty is, I know not, though it adheres to many things.' Dürer believed art was a way to find beauty in the most ordinary aspects of life."

"Like your drawing, James," Karl said gently. "Taking that ordinary scene outside your window and turning it into something beautiful."

James blushed, his freckles dark on his cheeks. But his face filled with a shy smile.

Christina continued to stare at the drawing. "Like any artist, Dürer put his life everywhere in his work. These drawings were a response to his own sadness and loneliness."

Karl frowned. "That's quite an assumption to make."

Christina raised an eyebrow. "Assump-

tion? We know a lot about his life from his letters."

"I don't doubt it, but you're assuming that his drawings are about his own life. The sadness you see could be a deliberate choice for this picture . . . something Dürer wanted to say about justice."

Marvin looked from one to the other. What were they going on about now? James's even-tempered father suddenly seemed annoyed.

Christina dismissed the comment, turning to James. "Whatever the reason, there's always this intense, lonely quality in Dürer's art. Do you see it?"

Marvin wanted a closer look at the drawing. There was something powerful about the picture, but also something held back. *Justice.*

"This picture wasn't with the others," James said.

"No. . . . No, it wasn't." Christina exchanged a glance with Denny.

Karl checked his watch. "Is that it, then? Is this all you wanted to show us?"

Christina's brow furrowed. "What I wanted to show *James,* yes."

Marvin looked at them in bewilderment. He'd never seen Karl show such dislike for someone, and it seemed fully reciprocated.

Christina crouched next to the table, her pretty face eye-level with James's. "James, have you ever tried to copy something? Just the way you copied the scene outside your window? But not a scene, a drawing."

"You mean, like, trace it?" James asked.

Christina shook her head. "No, not tracing. Copying the image yourself, just by studying the artist's lines."

"No," James said. "Well, I mean, sometimes . . . with cartoons. . . ." His voice trailed off.

"Do you think you could try with a Dürer drawing?"

James looked puzzled. "This one?"

"No," Christina said quickly. "Not this one. The one from Denny's museum that's hanging in the gallery. *Fortitude* —"

"What are you talking about?" Karl interrupted. "What would be the point of that?" He turned from Christina to Denny.

Denny himself looked unsure. "You want him to copy *Fortitude*? Why?"

"I don't know," Christina said softly. "It's probably hopeless. I just thought we'd see if he could make a good likeness of it."

"What — now? Here?" Karl shook his head. "I told you, we just came to see the exhibit. We don't have time for James to start sketching things."

James had a panic-stricken look on his face, and Marvin could feel him trembling. "All my drawing stuff is at home," he said.

Christina straightened, resting her slender hand on the edge of the table. "That's okay. If you'd prefer to take a copy of it home with you, that's fine." She flipped a page of the book. "Look, here it is, right after the *Justice* picture. You could take the whole book. I just — if you don't mind, James, I'd love to see if you could do it."

She hesitated, still watching James. "Nobody looked as closely at the world as Dürer. Nobody cared as much about capturing its smallest details. Your drawing has that same sensibility."

Marvin felt his heart swell.

Karl shook his head. "Dürer can't compare to Leonardo or Michelangelo."

Christina tilted her head, considering. "No, not in the emotional force of the drawings. He didn't have their originality and vision. He's a quieter artist. But in sheer patience . . ." She hesitated.

"Yes," Denny echoed firmly. "In his faith that beauty reveals itself, layer upon layer, in the smallest moments — well, there's no one like him."

"In truth, beauty . . . in beauty, truth." Christina reached her hand across the table and gently turned the pages back to the drawing *Justice.*

Denny slapped James's shoulder. "So what do you say, James? I'm not exactly sure what our mysterious Ms. Balcony is planning, but want to give it a try?"

Marvin couldn't take his eyes off the drawing: the strong solitary woman, with her sword at her side and the brass scales dangling from one hand. He wanted to draw like this. He wanted to be inside the head of Albrecht Dürer, adding each particular detail, getting closer and closer to the truth.

He knew what his parents would say. He

knew what his entire family would say. It was dangerous, ridiculous even.

But more than anything, he wanted James to say yes.

"I don't know," James said. "I don't know if I can."

"Will you try?" Christina's gaze was steady. "Please?"

James looked up at her, biting his lip. "Okay," he said finally.

"Oh, James! Thank you!" She bent quickly and hugged him. Just for a moment, her glossy golden head dipped close to Marvin, and he could smell the clean, warm scent of her skin.

Then she gasped. "OH, MY GOODNESS! A BUG!"

LEFT BEHIND

Marvin tried to dive out of sight, but before he could even register what was happening he felt a blow so forceful that it sent his entire body hurtling through space. He was upside down, turning in midair, the room a blur around him. He bounced off something hard — a wall? a bookshelf? Who could tell? — and crashed to the floor, where he lay on his back, legs waving.

"Where is he?" James cried.

"It's okay, I brushed it off," Christina said reassuringly. "But that was the strangest thing. It was right by your neck, under your collar. And in the winter too. Ugh!"

"But where did he go?"

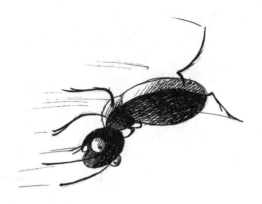

Marvin couldn't see anything from his inverted position. He pedaled his legs frantically, trying to heave himself upright.

"I have no idea," Christina said. "On the floor somewhere. It's probably dead."

"WHAT?" Marvin heard James's sneakers on the wood nearby.

"Take it easy, buddy," Karl said. "It's only a bug."

Marvin was afraid he'd be seen, afraid he'd be stepped on. There was nothing more vulnerable in the world than a beetle on its back. He twisted and turned, desperately trying to flip himself. This was something he and Elaine had practiced at home, with varying degrees of success. He was much better at it than Elaine, he reminded himself, summoning his last shred of strength.

Fortitude, he thought grimly.

With a mighty heave, he threw himself over. He landed on his belly and ran across the floorboards . . . under the table, out of sight. Phew!

From the shadows, Marvin could see four pairs of shoes. James's were anxiously jittering.

Karl crossed the room toward the door. "Let's go, James. We barely have time to see the rest of the exhibit."

James stayed where he was. "But —"

"Come on, buddy."

Christina's black pumps tapped across the floor to James's sneakers. "Do you want to take the book with you?"

"No!" James burst out, then added quickly, "I want to do it here. Is that okay, Dad? Can we come back tomorrow?"

He doesn't want to leave me, Marvin realized gratefully. *He's making sure he'll have to come back.*

"Tomorrow? The museum is closed on Monday."

"Yes, the exhibit halls are," Christina said, "but not the offices. Actually, that would work out perfectly. You could come after school if you like, James. And I'll make sure you have my office to yourself."

"Now wait a minute," Karl protested. "I

have no idea what his mother's plans are
—"

"Well, of course you'll have to check that
he doesn't have any other commitments,"
Christina said smoothly.

"I don't have any other commitments,"
James said. He crouched down, and Marvin
could see his pale, serious face squinting at
the floor. *Over here,* Marvin wanted to yell,
not that it would have done any good. He
tried to calculate whether he had enough
time to run across the floor and climb onto
James's sneaker without being seen.

"It's up to your mother." Karl paused.
"But she isn't likely to say yes if you're late
getting back today."

James sighed. "Okay, okay. I'll come
tomorrow," he said, a little too loudly.

Marvin saw the black pumps pivot. "Here,
James," Christina said. "Take one of my
cards. Call me and let me know when you'll
be here." Her voice lowered, and Marvin
could tell she was leaning down, speaking
only to James. "I'm so excited about this.
I'll tell you more about the drawings tomorrow."

"About this one?" James asked. *"Justice?"*

"Yes, and the others."

Marvin saw Denny's shoes move to the
door. "I can't wait to hear this," he said.

"Maybe then we'll know what you're up to."

"James," Karl said impatiently.

"Okay, Dad," James answered. Marvin watched the sneakers turn and trail reluctantly behind Karl's scuffed loafers. All four pairs of shoes drifted into the hallway, the light went off, and the door closed with a thud.

Marvin huddled in the dark. He listened to their footsteps echoing down the hall until the room was silent.

His parents would be crazy with worry, not knowing where he was. But what could he do about that now? James would be back tomorrow, Marvin felt sure of it. There was a connection between them, more than just the drawing. He knew James felt it too. Even though they'd only officially met that morning, it seemed as if they had known each other a long time. There was some mysterious click of understanding. Marvin had never felt that with anyone before.

He crawled out from under the table and climbed one of its massive wooden legs. The book lay open in front of him, smelling faintly of mildew, a comforting musty odor that made Marvin think of the water-softened walls of home. He crept across its satiny pages and stopped at the edge of the

Justice drawing. There, he settled down for the night, memorizing every line.

In Christina's Office

Just as the morning sunlight slanted through the large windows, Marvin heard a clatter out in the hallway. Moments later, a stoop-shouldered custodian wearing a brown coverall pushed through the door. He dragged a large trash can and a bucket of cleaning supplies. Marvin flattened himself, diving into the hollow between the bound pages and the book's thick cover. From there, he watched the custodian run his broom lazily over the floor, scooping a small pile of dust and debris into the trash, then wiping the tabletop disinterestedly with a rag. He didn't bother to move the book, so Marvin was safe.

Once the office was empty again, Marvin began to explore. He crawled down the table leg to the floor and then over to the far wall, quickly ascending to the window-sill. The view of the park was dizzyingly panoramic. Marvin could see feathery gray clusters of trees and thin asphalt paths cutting through winter grass. In the distance, people bundled in dark coats hurried away on their morning business, insignificant specks. *This must be what beetles look like to humans,* Marvin thought.

He crawled along the sill to Christina's desk, the surface of which was mostly bare, except for two neat stacks of paper, a canister of pens and pencils, a clock, and a silver-framed photograph. The photo was of Christina sitting on a sofa, feet tucked under her, with two little girls next to her. Or, really, Marvin thought, on top of her. One leaned across her lap, smiling up at her; the other was draped over her shoulders, one hand tangled possessively in her hair. Christina herself looked messy and rumpled, very unlike her appearance yesterday. But her face was shining. The girls had her delicate features and her same blond hair, only lighter. They must be her daughters, Marvin decided.

For the rest of the morning, he trekked around the office. He climbed the shelves and surveyed the stiff rows of books. He clung to the cord of the window shade and entertained himself by launching away from the wall and swinging slowly back and forth while the room gyrated below him. It was the closest he could come to flying, a skill shared by many other kinds of beetles — ladybugs, weevils — that Marvin and his family often envied.

In the early afternoon, he was pleased to find a thumbtack under the desk. If he'd been home, he would have promptly dragged it back to his collection, eager to show Elaine. Instead, he shoved it across the floor and hid it behind one of the table legs, feeling a bit more secure to know that a weapon was available should he have need of it.

After a while, Marvin grew hungry. He thought longingly of the substantial breakfast Mama and Papa would be enjoying right now, compliments of the Pompadays. Bagel with cream cheese? Pancake with maple syrup? The feast beneath William's high chair offered endless variety now that the baby was old enough to try different foods, but still young enough to enjoy throwing fistfuls onto the floor.

Marvin crawled over to the wastebasket by the file cabinet in the hope of finding a stray morsel. The custodian had banged it empty, but fortunately, his careless sweeping had scattered several crumbs under the desk. At first Marvin thought they were only bread crumbs — stale ones, he suspected, the leavings of a sandwich eaten days ago. But to his pure delight, he discovered tiny bits of a strawberry Pop-Tart.

As he gobbled the sweet pastry, Marvin felt considerably less inconvenienced by a day spent alone in Christina's office. With a full belly, he returned to the tabletop to look at the drawing again. The lines were delicate but unwavering. And how striking Justice was, with her sad face and her heavy sword. He wanted to draw this picture more than the one with the lion. He couldn't wait until James brought the ink.

Finally, hours later, Marvin heard keys in the lock. He concealed himself in the book's binding again, just as Christina came into the room, followed by James and then Karl, who stopped in the doorway. Christina was dressed as impeccably as the day before, in a crisp silk blouse and navy trousers, with her hair pulled smoothly away from her face and held in a tortoiseshell clasp. James, wide-eyed and nervous, shot quick glances in every direction, scanning the floor, the walls, the table. *He's looking for me,* Marvin thought happily.

"I'm so grateful you were able to come, James," Christina was saying, resting her hand on James's shoulder. "I know it must be difficult on a school day." She turned to Karl. "And you, too, Mr. Terik. I do realize it's an inconvenience for you."

"Well," Karl said, "James wanted to, so . . ." He shrugged and leaned awkwardly against the door frame.

Christina looked at James again. "Do you think you can work here at the table? If I clear off a space for you?" She scooted the stacks of paper aside, leaving a wide swath

of polished tabletop, with the large volume
of Dürer drawings in its center.

"Let's find *Fortitude*," she said, flipping
the pages. Marvin flinched and burrowed
deeper into the binding as the pages flut-
tered above him. "I see you brought your

ink set. Do you need paper? Anything else?"

James looked at the floor. "Just paper. But . . . I . . ." He stopped.

Christina crouched near him. "What is it?"

Marvin heard James scuff one sneaker against the floor. "I . . . I don't know if I can," he said in a small voice. "I don't know if I càn draw it here."

Christina nodded. "I completely understand. The artistic process is so . . . so *specific* for each person. For the great masters, it was too." She smiled encouragingly.

Karl was watching James. "It's a lot of pressure for a little guy," he said quietly.

Christina paused. "I don't mean it to be. Really, James, don't worry if it doesn't work. I'm sure there were times it didn't work for Dürer either."

Marvin saw Karl frown, and Christina reached out her hand quickly, resting it on his arm. He drew back in surprise, but she persisted. "Mr. Terik," she said, "I feel like you and I have gotten off to a bad start somehow. Can I buy you a cup of coffee? Please? To make up for your trouble coming all the way here again? It will give James a little peace while he works."

She smiled up at Karl, whose own face softened a little. "Okay," he said reluctantly.

"How long do you want, James? An hour? Hour and a half?"

James continued to scan the room, biting his lip. "Yeah. It could take me a while."

"Here's the paper," Christina said, setting a clean sheaf of heavy drawing paper on the table. "And here's *Fortitude.*" She traced her fingers over the girl wrestling the lion. "Just give it a try, James, okay?"

"Okay," James said, his cheeks pink.

They left, and as soon as the door clicked shut, James dropped to his knees, disappearing from Marvin's sight. Marvin could hear him whispering as he crawled around the floor. "Where are you? Where ARE you? Oh, please, please be okay!"

Marvin crawled out of the book's binding and scurried to the edge of the table. James continued to scramble across the floor, looking under the desk, peering into the rust-flaked grooves of the radiator. Marvin waited until he had dejectedly heaved to his feet and was staring around the room, then ran to the edge of the table, hoping that the flash of movement would attract the boy's attention.

"Hey!" James cried. "HEY! You're here!"

He collapsed in a chair and rested his chin on the table, inches from Marvin, his face split by a wide grin. He plunked his finger down. Marvin promptly crawled on top of it and held tight as James lifted him.

He had never seen James look so happy and relieved. *That's because James was worried about me,* he realized. *That's because we're friends.*

To Copy a Copy

"I'm so glad nothing happened to you, little guy," James said as he placed the paper in front of Marvin and shook the bottle of ink. "I mean, I kept thinking, 'What if he got stepped on?' Or, 'What if the janitor came and swept you up in the garbage?' "

Marvin thought this sounded like something Elaine would say.

But James continued happily, "I hope you can do this! I mean, she's totally counting on you. You know what this is like? This is like that fairy tale, the one with the girl and the straw. What's it called? . . . 'Rumpelstiltskin?'! Remember? Where the girl's locked in that room of the castle and she's supposed to spin the straw into gold or else they'll chop off her head?"

Marvin shuddered. No wonder human children found it entertaining to pull the legs off beetles, hearing stories like these. He crawled over to the drawing paper.

"And then that little elf or something comes and helps her, and nobody knows it," James finished. "Like you're helping me. Except it turns out the elf's kind of mean, and I can tell you're not mean. You're really, really nice." He took a deep breath.

"Okay, ready? Here's your ink." He unscrewed the cap, setting it down next to Marvin. "And what I'll do is, I'll put the book up like this" — he propped the huge volume upright, arranging other books on the table to hold it open — "so you can see it while you work, you know? Otherwise it'd be too hard; you'd have to crawl back and forth while you're drawing. This way, it's kind of like looking through the window in my room. Do you think you can do it?"

Well, that was the question, wasn't it? Marvin gazed at the drawing. James was right, it wasn't so different from looking through the bedroom window at the city street. Everything was there, in proportion; all he had to do was transfer it to the page.

But it was a drawing by a brilliant artist,

120

made hundreds of years ago! How could he copy something like that without messing up?

It didn't help to think that way, Marvin decided . . . just like it didn't help to think about the dark water in the drain, or what might be floating there when you were about to dive in. Your only hope was to stop thinking and do it.

He took a deep breath, dipped his front legs in the ink, and went to work.

The blank expanse of paper was overwhelming, but Marvin focused on an area the size of the drawing, marking the corners of an imaginary three-by-three-inch square with microscopic dots of ink. Then he began to draw. He concentrated on making his strokes as crisp and firm as Dürer's, without sacrificing the delicacy of the line. He started with the girl's tightly curled hair. Then he moved to the curve of her face.

James sat at the table with his arms crossed in front of him, his chin resting on them. Mostly he was silent, but sometimes he whispered encouragement: "Hey, good job," or "That part is tricky. . . . You can do it." Marvin nearly forgot James was there, so intent was he on the drawing. The girl took shape, her sturdy, muscled limbs bulging through the cloth of her gown. The lion

121

was easier somehow, its body held tight in the circle of human arms. Carefully, Marvin added the cross-hatching over its flank, then the flourish of its curling tail.

"That's *great*," James said in a low, breathless voice, as if afraid to break the spell.

Marvin discovered that if he copied individual parts of the drawing too mechanically, his lines seemed stiffer than Dürer's.

So he tried to capture the flow of the whole image. The hardest part was making his lines fluid and sure, as if he were drawing something new, all by himself, for the first time.

"Hey," James said suddenly, looking at the clock on Christina's desk. "It's almost five-thirty. They'll be back soon. Can you finish it?"

Marvin worked faster, slipping into the strange trance he'd felt when he first started sketching the scene outside James's window. It was a way of settling deep inside himself, lost to the outside world. He had no sense of anything but the page in front of him, the lines of ink blossoming into a picture.

Finally, the drawing was complete.

Marvin backed off the paper, holding his ink-stained legs aloft.

James nodded slowly, barely breathing. "It looks just like the other one!"

Marvin stared at it. It was all there: the crouching girl and her lion, every detail faithfully reproduced on the page. But was it as good as Dürer's? Marvin felt so much less certain of it than he had of his window drawing.

James, however, seemed perfectly confident. "They're not going to believe this," he said, grinning.

Minutes later, Karl, Christina, and Denny walked through the door. James had already secured Marvin in his jacket pocket to avoid a repeat of yesterday's scare. Marvin gripped the flap, anxiously watching Christina's reaction.

"Oh!" she gasped. "Oh, James!"

Denny laughed out loud.

Marvin couldn't tell if that was good or bad. Did they like it?

"Wow," said Karl, approaching the table.

James stepped backward, fiddling with the zipper on his jacket. Marvin looked up and saw the same pink flush creeping over his cheeks.

"James, this is *excellent*," Christina said, lifting the paper. "I can't believe it. I have to confess, I thought it was worth a try, but — Denny, look! Did you ever imagine he'd be able to do it so well?" She turned excitedly to Karl. "Did you?"

To his surprise, Marvin saw that the dynamic between them had entirely shifted, the prickly short-temperedness gone. Karl smiled at her, his face mirroring her enthusiasm.

"No! I thought he could get the line right, but copying something requires a different skill altogether. The proportions are really good here, James — the way you've got them in space. Hmmm. I think the overall effect in the Dürer is not quite so crowded, though. Do you agree?" Karl said this to Christina, who looked more closely at the image in the book.

Marvin saw what he meant. In the original, despite its miniature size, the girl and the lion formed a broad triangle in space.

"True," said Denny. "But it's very fine work. The technical command is extraordinary."

Christina nodded. "And this is his first try. *And* it's from a reproduction in an art book, not from the original drawing." She paused, shaking her head. "I'm almost afraid to say this, but it's given me hope."

Marvin glanced up at James, who clearly

125

shared his bewilderment. What was she talking about?

"Hope for what?" Karl asked.

"Yes, Christina, do tell," Denny added. "Your plans have been a mystery long enough. Why a copy of *Fortitude*? Still smarting because I outbid you on it at auction?"

Christina laughed at him. "No, no, I got over that a long time ago."

"Why then?" Denny persisted. "Why do you need a copy of *Fortitude*?"

Christina's eyes sparkled. "Because," she said slowly, her voice barely containing her excitement, "it's about to be stolen."

STEALING VIRTUE

"What?" cried Denny and Karl simultaneously. Marvin poked his head farther out of the pocket, almost toppling to the floor.

Christina smiled. "Not the real drawing! Don't worry. James's copy of it."

"I don't understand," Karl said.

Denny frowned, raking his hair back with one hand. "Nor do I. And since the real one belongs to the Getty, I think I'd better hear the details of this. Perhaps we should sit down."

Christina pulled out a chair and sank into it, placing the drawing in front of her, her slim hands flanking it on the table. Denny and Karl sat down on either side of her, but

James remained standing. *So I can see,* Marvin thought gratefully.

"Well," Christina began, "Denny's familiar with the background of all this, but I doubt you two are." She turned to Karl. "Know anything about art heists?"

"Sure," Karl said. "The famous ones. The *Mona Lisa.* The Gardner Museum in Boston."

"What?" asked James. "What are those?"

Christina took off her glasses and set them on the table, staring at the drawing. "The most famous art thefts of all time. The *Mona Lisa* was taken in 1911. An Italian workman took it from the Louvre, planning to return it to Italy. It was missing for two years, but they got it back." She rubbed her forehead. "The Isabella Stewart Gardner Museum wasn't so lucky. The biggest single art theft in history — in 1990, two men dressed as police officers arrived in the early morning, saying they were responding to a call. They handcuffed the security guards and stole three Rembrandts, a Vermeer, a Manet, and five Degas paintings, among others. The whole lot was worth almost four hundred million dollars. They've never been found."

"Wow," said James. Marvin thought of all those paintings, gone.

James looked at Christina. "But why do

people steal them? What do they do with them?"

Christina sighed. "Usually, it's for the money," she said. "But of course the paintings are often so well known, they can't be sold openly, at auction."

Denny nodded, rubbing his forehead. "The market in stolen art is a difficult one. Thieves can't sell to museums or reputable dealers. Any private collector who buys a stolen painting can't display it publicly. He'd have to want it for its own sake — just for the art — and be willing to enjoy it in private."

Christina nodded. "So it tends to be a

black-market business. . . . Criminals trade the paintings for other forbidden things, like drugs or guns."

"Really?" James's eyes were wide. Marvin had to admit, it was hard to picture someone swapping one of those lovely, delicate, centuries-old artworks for a secret stash of weapons.

"Well, that's one kind of theft," Denny interjected. "Stealing art is not like other crimes. Sometimes it's not for money at all. Sometimes it's really for love."

"True." Christina nodded. "There can be genuine feeling behind it. In the case of the *Mona Lisa,* the thief just wanted the painting returned to its homeland."

"But why would he care about that?" James asked.

Karl ruffled his hair. "It's Leonardo da Vinci's most famous work. Many Italians see it as a national treasure. They aren't happy that it's in a French museum."

"His works are common targets for thieves," Christina said. "*Madonna with the Yarnwinder* was taken from a Scottish castle several years ago, by two men posing as tourists. They overpowered a guide and took it right off the wall."

"Was that worth a lot of money too?" James asked.

"Oh, yes. It's a masterpiece. Fifty million? A hundred million? Never recovered."

James let out a long breath, and Marvin wasn't sure whether it was because of the lost money or the lost painting.

"Do they ever get them back? The paintings, I mean," he asked Christina.

"It's rare, but it happens. You can't imagine how exciting that is." She squeezed James's shoulder. "When Edvard Munch's painting *The Scream* was found, the museum opened its doors for a night and served champagne. Everyone in the art world was overjoyed. And then there was that strange theft in Manchester, right, Denny?" Christina turned to Denny for confirmation. "In England a few years ago, a bunch of stolen canvases by van Gogh, Picasso, and Gauguin were found rolled up in a cardboard tube and stuffed behind a public toilet, just down the street from the gallery where they'd been stolen two days earlier."

"Was the thief caught?" Karl asked.

Denny shook his head. "Not that I recall. And in that case, he left a nice little note complimenting the gallery on its security!" He smiled. "Again, it's not your typical crime, and the people involved aren't your typical criminals."

"Well," Christina protested, "sometimes they are. The National Museum in Stockholm? Three men with guns broke in and stole a Rembrandt self-portrait and two Renoirs."

"Yes, that's right," Denny murmured. "They escaped by speedboat. Those paintings were recovered by a Danish policeman posing undercover as an art buyer."

"Really?" Karl said. "They got all of them back?"

"Yes," Christina answered, lost in thought. "All of them."

The room fell silent. Marvin's head was spinning. It was hard to imagine dusty, quiet museums as the settings for such flamboyant crimes. It was also hard to believe that a drawing or painting could be worth so many millions of dollars.

"But what's all this got to do with the Dürer drawing?" Karl asked finally.

"There are four drawings, actually," Christina said, "of the four cardinal virtues: Fortitude, Justice, Prudence, and Temperance. Bellini drew only a picture of Fortitude, but Dürer drew pictures of all four. All miniatures, incredibly detailed."

"What does that mean . . . 'prudence'?" James asked.

His father paused. "Carefulness, really.

Being cautious, thinking things through."

That was like James, thought Marvin. James was always careful.

"And temperance is moderation," Christina explained. "Not overdoing it."

Marvin rolled his eyes, though no one could see him. Grown-ups couldn't seem to understand that it was always better to overdo it.

"Okay, four Dürer drawings," Karl prompted her. "And?"

"And . . . they were stolen. Or at least, three of them were. *Prudence* and *Temperance* were taken from a little museum in Baden-Baden, Germany, two years ago — they were so small, the thief just lifted the frames from the wall and tucked them under his jacket."

It would be easy to hide those drawings, Marvin thought. They were so little.

"*Justice* . . ." Christina hesitated.

Marvin saw that Denny was watching her, his expression a blend of sympathy and regret. When she didn't go on, he started talking himself: "*Justice* was taken last year. The Met had just purchased it, at Christina's urging, from a London dealer. It was a major coup for the collection. Old Master drawings have become a hot ticket lately, selling for hundreds of thousands. I wanted it for the Getty, of course." He smiled down at James. "A companion to *Fortitude*. My museum in California has quite a collection of European drawings, and I have a soft spot for Dürer. For the *Virtue* drawings in particular."

"*Justice* had minor water damage," Christina continued. "It was in the Conservation Department last March, being repaired, when the office was broken into. That drawing was the only thing taken." She shook her head at Denny.

"It was terrible," Denny said. "I was in New York for a conference, and the theft cast a pall over our entire weekend. We were all just stunned."

"I remember reading about it," Karl said. "But why only that drawing? There must have been other valuable artworks in Conservation."

Christina and Denny exchanged a wistful smile.

"Dürer," Denny said.

"Yes, Dürer," Christina agreed. "If it were just an ordinary theft — you're right, there were several valuable paintings in the office. But this wasn't about the money, in my opinion, nor were the thefts of the two other *Virtue* drawings, *Prudence* and *Temperance*. People have a thing for Dürer."

Karl raised an eyebrow.

But Marvin immediately understood. That was the power of the drawings: the sadness, homeliness even, of the people. They were so real.

James chewed his lip, studying Marvin's picture of the woman and the lion. "But I don't see why you need a copy of this one," he said. "You *have* this one. Why don't you want a copy of *Justice,* since that's the one that's missing?"

"Because, James," Christina said eagerly, her words soft and rushed, "I think someone is collecting these drawings. And whoever that person is, he'll want the complete set. The four virtues. This is the only one left." She turned to Denny. "I've been talking to people at the FBI, in the art-theft program. They say it might work. They're willing to help."

"Help what?" Karl exclaimed in frustration. "I still don't understand."

James dropped into a chair, and Marvin was immediately blocked from any view of the adults. He inched his way out of the pocket and climbed James's zipper surreptitiously, glad that everyone's attention was focused elsewhere.

Christina took a deep breath. "Okay, okay. I'm sorry. I know it's complicated. But everything is almost in place!" She looked at Denny. "I have the support of the FBI. They have an underground contact, someone who deals in stolen art. What I need is a forgery of *Fortitude*."

"But why?" James asked.

Christina twisted her hands together, her face flushed. "This is my plan: We'll have you draw it again, James, on the right paper with the right ink. Then we'll substitute your drawing for the real one, and stage a theft. Listen, the drawing has to be good, but it doesn't have to be perfect. Everyone knows *Fortitude* is part of this exhibition. They know it's real. Our forgery won't be judged for authenticity by the thief, only by the person intending to buy it . . . and that deal will never happen."

"What thief?" Karl asked. "This isn't making sense. You're going to hire someone to steal your own drawing?"

"The forgery. Not the real one. And the 'thief' will be someone who works for the FBI." She paused. "They'll put some kind of tracking device on the fake drawing of *Fortitude*. The FBI will get the drawing into the hands of someone who deals in stolen art —"

"And that person will lead you to the other drawings," Denny finished. He nod-

ded slowly. "To *Justice*. It's very clever."

It *was* clever, Marvin thought. Who'd suspect a museum of masterminding its own burglary? Of forging its own art?

Karl shook his head. "But how do you get the drawing to the black market? That's not exactly easy. It's not like you have regular contact with criminals." He raised his eyebrows, adding, "I assume."

"No," Christina allowed. "But remember what Denny said about the Stockholm theft? The undercover policeman? That's been one of the most effective ways to recover stolen art: police officers or FBI agents posing as underground art dealers. I feel sure we can get the forgery into the right hands." She smiled. "Or the wrong hands, as the case may be."

"My hat's off to you, Christina," Denny said. "It's impressive."

"So you're going to pretend to steal my drawing?" James asked.

Christina nodded.

"But what if you're wrong?" Karl asked. "What if there isn't one person who is collecting the complete set? What if the drawings aren't together?"

"Well, that's always a possibility."

"And what if something happens to my drawing?" James asked. In his spot on James's jacket, Marvin shuddered. His drawing . . . would it disappear into this world of fake policemen and guns and million-dollar paintings lost forever?

Christina knelt beside James, inches from Marvin, who quickly hid himself in a fold of fabric. "The whole thing is a gamble. I know that," she said gently, looking only at James. Marvin realized this was one of the things he liked about Christina: how she gave James her full attention, as though anything he said or asked was every bit as important as the comments coming from the grown-ups.

"The FBI doesn't care," she continued,

"whether our staged burglary leads to the stolen Dürer drawings or to other stolen works of art. It will still point the way to key players in the underground art market. But, of course, *I* care. If this doesn't give us *Justice,* I'll be . . ." — she hesitated — "so disappointed."

Karl still looked uncertain. "I see how it could work, but won't you need a lot of other people on board? I mean, the museum security staff, the New York City police, the papers —"

"Well, not the papers," Denny interrupted. "I assume it's important for the press to report this as if it were a real theft."

"Yes," Christina agreed. "It has to look like a real burglary from the outside. But, Karl, you're right about the others. I have to get permission from the director of the Met and make sure the local police are willing to help. That's why the involvement of the FBI is important. And Denny, I want you to clear it with the Getty, too, obviously, since it's one of your loaned pieces that's the center of the whole plan. The thing is . . ."

Christina kept staring at James, her eyes filled with wonder. "This idea occurred to me months ago, when Denny and I were discussing the setup for the exhibit. But I never thought I'd find someone who could do the forgery of *Fortitude.* I didn't believe it was possible . . . until I saw your drawing, James. And then I thought: 'He could do it.' And you did!"

Marvin felt a strange mixture of pride and fear and worry. James only blushed, staring at the drawing.

"Okay," he said quietly. "You want me to copy it so you can steal it."

"Yes," Christina agreed. "Steal the fake one to find the real one. *Justice.*"

HITCHING A RIDE

It was nearly seven o'clock by the time Karl, James, and Marvin returned to the Pompadays' apartment and provided Mrs. Pompaday with a plausible (but not too detailed) explanation of why James would need to make another visit to the Met that week. Karl described it as a private art tutorial with the Curator of Drawings and Prints, which managed to satisfy Mrs. Pompaday's hankerings for special treatment, recognition of her child's distinction, and entrée into an exclusive world of upper-class pursuits, all at once. They agreed that Karl would come for James on Wednesday at four o'clock.

When James finally retreated to the sanctuary of his bedroom, Marvin was frantic to return to the bosom of his own family. They would be beside themselves with worry. He'd been gone overnight — again! — and the whole of the next day, and there was no way for them to know what had transpired. He hoisted himself over the lip of the jacket pocket and began to scurry down the boy's pants leg to the floor. James stopped him with a finger.

"Here," he said, "let me help. I don't know where you're going, but it's out in the hall somewhere, right? That's where you live?"

Marvin sighed. How wonderful it would be if he could just explain to James where home was and hitch a ride straight there. It would take James mere seconds to cross the apartment to the kitchen cupboard, compared to the half hour or more it would take Marvin. Here was a truly bothersome inconvenience of being friends with someone you couldn't communicate with in any of the usual ways.

But maybe James would figure something out. It seemed worth a try. At least he'd get as far as the hall. Marvin crawled onto James's knuckle and held tight as the boy walked to the doorway.

"Don't worry," James said. "I'll make sure

nobody sees." He cracked the door and looked both ways. They could hear William bellowing in the kitchen. "Ya ya! Ya ya!"

"I'm coming, William," James called, smiling a little. James was unaccountably patient with William, Marvin thought, submitting to his hair-pulling, picking up his dropped toys. None of the beetles could understand it.

"My mom's fixing dinner," James said to Marvin. "It's okay." He crouched and laid his finger on the smooth polished floor, next to the baseboard. "Here?" He watched Marvin.

Marvin started to climb down, but then James said, "Hey! Know what? If you crawl to the end of my finger when I'm in the right spot, I can put you down *exactly* where you need to be." He squatted back on his heels, grinning. "It'll be like that game Hot-or-Cold, you know?"

Marvin beamed up at him. James was so smart. He settled himself in the middle of James's finger and held on as the boy wandered down the hallway, pausing every few minutes and watching for Marvin's reaction. Marvin sat tight.

James stepped into the bathroom, then poked his head into his parents' room. *Not here,* Marvin thought, shuddering. He

couldn't imagine spending any more time than was absolutely necessary with Mr. and Mrs. Pompaday. What a racket they made with their constant chatter, not to mention the frequent explosions.

"Huh," James said. "I hope you get what I mean. You don't seem to be doing anything. Listen, if I'm *not* close to where you live, crawl the other way, down my finger toward my hand, okay?"

Marvin obligingly crawled toward James's hand.

James laughed out loud.

"James, is that you? What's so funny?" Mrs. Pompaday stuck her head around the doorway from the kitchen. James immediately dropped his hand to his side, and Marvin held on for dear life.

"Nothing," James said. "I just saw something funny."

Mrs. Pompaday looked at him suspiciously. "Out here in the hall? I hope you weren't laughing at my Apsara statue." Marvin watched her cross to the hall table and tenderly lift a small hand-carved wooden figurine of a naked woman dancing. "I noticed some of your little friends laughing at her during the party, but I trust you're more mature than that. The female body is a beautiful thing, James."

James squirmed. "I wasn't laughing at that, Mom."

"Well, good, because you're an *artist* now, dear. You need to show appreciation for the art of different cultures . . . even those silly old Eskimo sculptures your father has lying around. Why, when I think that your pretty drawings might be hanging in somebody's

parlor — oh, it just gives me goose bumps!"
She swooped down and kissed the top of
James's head.

James stiffened in surprise and slid his
hand behind his leg, shielding Marvin.
"When's dinner?" he asked, clearly desperate to change the subject.

"Twenty minutes." Mrs. Pompaday returned to the kitchen.

James walked toward the living room.
"We're almost out of rooms, little guy.
Here?" He paused in the middle of the

Oriental rug, looking around. Marvin stayed close to his hand.

"See my dad's horse painting?" James asked softly. "Isn't it great?" He walked closer, leaning over the couch to stare at it. Marvin leaned toward it, too, balancing lightly on his rear legs. The painting was bold and graceful, with its rush of bright blue color. You would never know it was a horse unless someone told you. But once you knew it was a horse, it was impossible to see it as anything else.

James glanced down at Marvin. "Do you think I'll ever be able to make something like that? Probably not." He sighed. "I mean, I can't even draw. You're the one who can."

Marvin looked up at him sympathetically.

"But not without my ink set, right?" James said, smiling suddenly. "So it *is* like you need my help." He looked at his father's canvas again. "But could you make a painting? I don't think so. Not one this big, anyway. It would take you years! We'd better stick to the small stuff."

Marvin realized it was possible to have an entire conversation with James without saying a word. There were beetles like that, who did all the talking . . . but with James, it was like he did the listening, too, and filled in the gaps with what he knew you would say if only you could.

"Okay. Dining room?" James drifted thoughtfully through the archway. Marvin stayed put. "Huh. I don't think you live in William's room. Did I tell you William ate a ladybug once? Yep, he did. Picked it up and popped it right in his mouth. My mom totally freaked out." Marvin shuddered as James continued. "Let's try the kitchen, but we have to be careful because everybody's in there."

As they turned to the kitchen, Marvin inched toward the middle of James's finger. James grinned. "Okay! Getting hotter!" he whispered, tiptoeing into the room.

Mrs. Pompaday was busy at the stove, stirring something with a metal spoon. Marvin crawled to the end of James's finger and James swiftly bent and deposited him on the tile floor, close to the wall of cupboards. Delighted at the ease and speed of the journey home, Marvin darted gratefully into the shadows.

"James," Mrs. Pompaday protested, "don't sneak up on me like that, I almost tripped over you. And what are you doing down there on the floor?"

"Tying my shoelace," James mumbled,

just as Marvin disappeared inside the kitchen cupboard.

Too Risky

When Marvin came through the front door, his mother burst into tears. "Oh, Marvin, darling! Where on earth were you?"

"I'm sorry, Mama —" Marvin began, but before he could finish, she smothered him in a hug, covering his shell with several legs at once.

His father hurried over, clearing his throat gruffly. "Marvin, you've had us worried out of our shells! Why didn't you come home yesterday? You got me in a lot of trouble with your mother, I hope you realize, for ever allowing you to stay behind."

"We went to a museum —"

"A museum! What?" Mama's eyes widened. "You left the apartment? Marvin, you have no business doing human things like that. It's too dangerous! I know you want to help James, but not at the risk of your own life. Why, your father and Uncle Albert made trip after trip to James's room, looking for you. We had no idea what had happened!"

"I'm sorry," Marvin said again. He explained about the drawings at the Met, the visit to Christina's office, and the surprise of being knocked to the floor and left there.

"Oh!" Mama cried. "Darling, you're lucky you're still alive! What were you doing there, anyway?"

Marvin sighed. So much had happened since yesterday. How could he make his parents understand? "I'm hungry," he said. "Could we talk about it at dinner?"

Mama nodded. "Yes, yes, of course, you must be starving. Here, sit down and eat something. It's been a long day, for all of us."

So the three beetles gathered around the rectangular pink eraser that served as their kitchen table, and Mama heaped it with foil platters of hearty digestibles: tiny steaming broccoli florets from the Pompadays' supper, two cubes of cheddar from William's lunch, crispy brown chicken skin, a lemon

rind, a crushed potato chip, and a cherry Life Savers for dessert. Marvin hungrily devoured every morsel, and between mouthfuls haltingly relayed the story of Dürer, the missing *Virtue* drawings, his own effort to copy *Fortitude,* and Christina's plan to stage a theft from the museum.

His parents were so astonished they stopped eating halfway through the meal and just listened. When Marvin was finished, Papa shook his head. "Well, that is amazing. Faking the theft of their own picture, huh?"

"Not the real picture, though," Marvin

said. "My copy of it."

Mama smiled at him. "I'm sure it was lovely, Marvin. I wish I could have seen it! But humans lead such complicated lives, don't they? Why would people steal something they couldn't sell or even hang on their own wall?"

Marvin hesitated. He understood that, somehow. "Maybe just to have it. Because it's so beautiful . . . then you could look at it whenever you wanted."

"Well, I don't think it makes sense," Mama said. "And it's wrong."

"Humans are masters at making their own trouble," Papa agreed.

"I'm just glad you're home safe, Marvin. It's time to put all this behind you."

Marvin hesitated. "I can't, Mama."

"What do you mean?"

"Christina Balcony, the woman at the museum, needs James to make another copy of *Fortitude*. A really good one . . . which means he needs me."

"To do another drawing?" Mama shook her head vigorously. "Darling, no! You simply can't. It's too risky."

"Your mother's right, Marvin," Papa chimed in. "The family didn't like this from the beginning. We wanted you to get rid of your drawing altogether, remember? You can't get more involved. It's dangerous for everyone."

"But —"

"I'm sorry, Marvin. I know you want to help James," his mother said gently. "You tried your best. But it's time to let the humans work this out on their own."

"Mama, please," Marvin protested. "You don't understand. James can't do the drawing himself. He's counting on me."

Mama took Marvin's leg firmly and led him toward the bedroom. "What I understand is that this has gone on long enough. It's an elaborate deceit, that's what it is. For a good purpose or not, it's still wrong. Don't you remember the saying, 'Oh what a tangled web we weave when first we practice to deceive'?"

Marvin rolled his eyes. "Mama, that's a

spider saying."

"It applies just as well here. You're helping James to mislead people. You've been missing twice overnight, under circumstances that could have gotten you badly hurt or even killed. Enough, darling. It's time for bed. I'm sure you're exhausted after your adventure at the museum."

"But, Mama —"

"Good night, Marvin. Sleep tight, don't let the bedbugs bite." She nestled him in his cotton-ball bed, kissed his shell, and left the room.

Marvin lay on his side, wide awake, staring at the wall. Today was Monday. James was supposed to return to the museum after school on Wednesday to do the new drawing. He thought of the boy hovering over the blank page, with no idea what to do. How could Marvin abandon him? This was the very heart of friendship, Marvin thought — your willingness to help each other in a jam, to take a friend's problems as your very own.

Marvin sighed. He had to think of something before Wednesday afternoon, or James would be in big trouble.

IN THE SOLARIUM

Marvin slept late the next morning, exhausted from the events of the last few days. When he finally awoke, his mother was at his bedside, smiling.

"Marvin, Papa and I thought of a nice outing for you today, something to take your mind off things. Edith, Albert, and Elaine are going to join us for a picnic in the solarium. We haven't been there in weeks, and it will lift your spirits, darling. The maids are coming at nine, though, so you have to get ready now."

At the far end of the Pompadays' apartment was a small, bright, glassed-in sunporch filled with flowering plants. It was the beetles' only regular experience of nature, and it was especially appealing in winter, when the exotic greenery and sweet-smelling blossoms offered respite from the cold gray days unfolding beyond the apartment windows. Since it was too far for an easy day trip, the beetles usually waited till Tuesdays when the maids came, catching a ride on the underside of the vacuum-cleaner canister. The maids were in the regular habit of cleaning the kitchen first and then the solarium, because they both sported tile floors that required a particular vacuum attachment.

Usually the prospect of a day in the solarium would have thrilled Marvin, since it was a veritable amusement park for young beetles. But today it just seemed a distraction from more important pursuits. "Okay," he said glumly, still thinking about James and the drawing.

"Oh, Marvin, please! Cheer up. It will be fun. Have a bite of breakfast quickly — bacon this morning! James must have missed the trash can when he scraped his plate — and we'll get going. Look . . . Elaine is here already."

His mother returned to the kitchen, and Marvin rolled out of bed, rubbing his eyes as his cousin poked her head around the doorway.

"Marvin! I can't believe you went to the museum without me! It sounds fantastic. Well, scary, of course. I mean, VERY scary, what with you getting swatted by that woman and everything. Good thing she didn't squash you flat. What if she mistook you for a mosquito? Ka-POW! You'd be dead meat right now."

Marvin frowned at her. "I know."

"I wish I'd been with you! You know how I'm dying to see the world. I never get to leave this old place. Borrrrring."

Marvin felt a vague twinge of sympathy. It was certainly a good thing to be safe, but it could be tedious in its way too. You always wondered what you were missing. A little danger was worth it just to mix things up, to add some surprise to life. *A little* danger, he thought.

Marvin bolted down his breakfast, and then he, Elaine, Aunt Edith, Uncle Albert, Mama, and Papa all made their way out of the cupboard to their preferred waiting spot for a vacuum-cleaner ride: the underlip of the dishwasher. Hidden from view, they stood patiently until the maids had finished vacuuming the kitchen floor. As soon as the two women turned to collect their cleaning supplies, the six beetles dashed toward the vacuum-cleaner canister, scrambled up one dusty wheel, and dove for cover under its hard metal belly. Between them, Papa and Uncle Albert awkwardly balanced the picnic hamper, which was fashioned from the fingertip of a yellow rubber glove. It was bulging with food, tied shut with a bit of twine.

One of the maids gave the vacuum cleaner a tug, and it scooted easily across the kitchen floor, through the hallway, and across the living-room rug to the solarium. There, she paused to unlatch the French doors, then dragged the canister over the door saddle and bumped it onto the terra-cotta tile. This was the roughest part of the journey, and inevitably one of the beetles nearly fell off. Today it was Mama, who had released her grip on the canister momentarily to tighten the hamper's twine. "My dear, hold on!" Papa bellowed, grabbing the edge of her shell at the last minute.

And so they all made it safely to the solarium. They dropped off the canister and hid beneath it until they were sure the maids were distracted, and then darted across the floor. It was always a challenge to keep the picnic hamper out of sight during this part of the trip. Even though it was tiny by human standards, its bright yellow color at-

tracted attention. Quickly, Mama and Aunt Edith led the way up the leg of one of the plant stands — a staggered series of shelves framed in ornate wrought-iron scrollwork, laden with flowering plants.

As soon as they reached the top, Elaine scurried off, pulling Marvin with her. "We're going exploring," she yelled.

"Meet us in the herb garden for lunch," Mama called after them. "We'll have a nice oregano salad with our picnic. Around noon, okay?"

"Okay, Mama," Marvin answered, diving under a lavender mum with Elaine.

The solarium was full of diverting entertainment for Marvin and Elaine. Elaine liked to start at the box of geraniums, where

Mrs. Pompaday kept her metal gardening spade. The spade was usually leaning against the wall, tilted at the perfect angle to be used as a slide. Today, they climbed up the wall to where its wooden handle rested, delicately reached across and secured footing there, then shinnied down to the metal trough.

"You first," Elaine announced. She never liked to go until she'd been reassured that there were no unpleasant surprises at the bottom, where the tip of the spade disappeared into the crumbly earth. Once, the spade had been propped against the base of

a geranium, and Elaine, not noticing, had whooshed down the slide directly into the woody stalk, hitting it head-on and almost knocking herself out.

Marvin climbed into position, gripping the edge of the spade with his two hind legs. "Here I go . . ." he said.

He let go of the metal and shot down the spade like a bullet.

"Whooooooooooooooooo," he yelled, whizzing through space, the geraniums a blur of orange and green at the periphery of his vision.

"Pick up your legs, you'll go faster," Elaine called after him.

Just before he hit bottom, Marvin launched himself off the spade and into the air, sailing over the soil and landing in one of the geranium blooms.

"That was awesome!" Elaine cried delightedly. "My turn — watch this!"

She flipped onto her back and, with legs waving gaily in the air, soared down the slide even faster than Marvin had . . . although, he noted, she had insufficient leverage to fly off the bottom, so she crashed instead, thudding into the earthen hollow at the base of the spade.

"Good one," he called approvingly.

"Let's do a train," Elaine suggested.

They climbed to the top of the spade and linked themselves, with Marvin's hind legs grasping Elaine's front ones, and off they went, faster than fast with their double weight propelling them down the slide.

They spent most of the morning coming up with variations on this theme: the double-decker (one on top of the other), the spinning teacup (both sitting upright, with all six legs linked), the double belly flop (side by side, front legs touching, launching off the top of the spade into midair). Finally, they sunk into the soft earth, thoroughly exhausted.

"Is it lunchtime yet?" Elaine wanted to know. "I'm starving."

"Me too," Marvin replied. "But look at

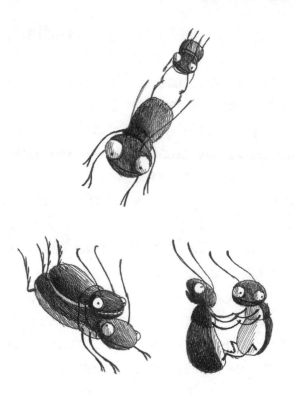

the clock."

The blue and green wall clock, decorated with a ceramic relief of morning glories, hung on the opposite wall between the large windows. Marvin could see that its vine-ensconced hands exactly divided the face. The beetles had worked out the basics of telling time from long observation of the big clock on the kitchen wall — it was handy to keep track of Pompaday meal-times. While Marvin couldn't identify numbers, he knew that the clock's hands would both be pointing straight up at noon.

"We have a little while longer," he told Elaine.

"Hmmm," said Elaine. "I know! Let's see what the turtle is up to." She gave Marvin a challenging look. Technically, they were not supposed to go anywhere near the turtle aquarium, as Elaine knew full well. Both Mama and Aunt Edith deemed it entirely too dangerous.

Marvin hesitated. As long as they stayed outside the glass, what harm could there be? The turtle was sluggish and indifferent to visitors anyway, unlikely to notice them.

"Okay," Marvin said.

"Really?" Elaine squealed in delight. "I was sure you'd say no. I think you're getting braver, Marvin."

She thumped his shell approvingly and scuttled across the geranium bed, along the wrought-iron shelf, then down one leg of the plant stand to the floor. Marvin followed her, glancing around to make sure the maids were gone. It never took them long to clean the solarium, but they always left the French doors open for a while to air the room out. Mrs. Pompaday would close them in the evening, when the beetles had long since returned home. On rare occasions, Mama and Papa organized a camping trip, and the whole family stayed overnight. But the grown-ups were always careful to watch the human comings and goings, because, as Papa noted, the last thing they needed was for the Pompadays to spy a beetle and decide to wage a wholesale fumigation campaign in this pleasant vacation spot. That might ruin it for good.

"The coast is clear," Marvin told her.

"Go behind the table," Elaine urged. "So our parents won't see us."

Marvin led the way behind the large wooden table where the turtle aquarium rested in the center, surrounded by small flowerpots of orchids and violets. He climbed up the plaster wall, over the lip of the table, and along the polished surface to the glass corner of the aquarium. The tank was half-filled with murky green water. It had a large flat rock on one side — with a shallow plastic food bowl in the middle of it — where the turtle climbed out to sun himself when he wasn't swimming. He was rarely swimming, it seemed to Marvin, and today, true to form, he was hunched impassively on the edge of the rock, next to the food bowl.

"He's not doing much," Marvin noted.

"Oh, he never is, is he?" Elaine scoffed. "Boring old thing." She climbed a few inches up the side of the glass. "Let's see if we can get his attention."

"Elaine," Marvin said, worried. "I don't think you should do that."

"Come on, it's perfectly safe. I'm on the outside."

"I know, but we're not even supposed to be over here." Marvin peered in either direction nervously. If one of the grown-ups saw Elaine climbing the side of the aquarium, there would certainly be a to-do.

"Are you coming?" Elaine asked impatiently.

Marvin sighed. Reluctantly, he climbed a couple of inches up the glass. It was slippery and cool underfoot.

Elaine was several inches above him, waving her legs at the turtle. "Yoo-hoo! Over here, you big lug . . . heads up! Look sharp!"

The turtle didn't budge.

"Oh, honestly. He's blind as a bat." Elaine crawled toward the top edge of the aquarium.

"Elaine, don't," Marvin protested. "You're too close. You'll fall in."

"No, I won't," Elaine retorted. "Besides, it wouldn't matter if I did. That turtle is too old and too tired and too dumb to care."

Marvin climbed a little farther. As he was approaching the middle of the wall, he saw a flash of something — so quick he wasn't

167

sure he'd seen it — and then *thunk!* The side of the aquarium shook with a force that threw him to the ground.

Why, that sly old thing, Marvin thought. The turtle must have spotted him after all. He'd lunged at the wall of the tank, not realizing Marvin was on the other side, out of reach, and now thrashed through the water along the wall of the tank, his sleek head moving back and forth.

"Did you see that?" Marvin called to Elaine. He crawled back up the wall of glass. When she didn't answer, he looked up.

Elaine was nowhere to be seen.

"Elaine!" Marvin shouted. Maybe when the turtle rammed the glass she'd fallen over backward too. He clung to the glass and looked around, scanning the round, furry leaves of the violets, the pale orchid blossoms. "Elaine, where are you?"

Still no response. Marvin, increasingly frantic, climbed farther up the side of the aquarium for a better view. "Elaine!"

Then he saw her. She was floating on her

back in the water below, perfectly still, while the turtle dove and surfaced nearby.

TURTLE-BEETLE BATTLE

She must have toppled over the edge when the turtle struck the glass.

"Elaine, don't move!" Marvin cried to her. "Don't make any noise! He doesn't see you yet. I'm coming."

Thank goodness she was on her back, Marvin thought, because Elaine was definitely not a swimmer. On her back, at least she could float . . . but she couldn't do anything to save herself. And with the turtle careening through the water like that, it was only a matter of time till he saw her.

Marvin dashed around the rim of the tank, his eyes never leaving his cousin. When he reached the back of the aquarium, he

cautiously climbed over the edge and started down the inside wall. He was too high up for the turtle to see him, but he had to make it all the way down the side unnoticed.

Elaine was staring up at Marvin with huge frightened eyes. The turtle glided and dipped through the water, inches away, his long glistening neck thrashing back and forth like a sea monster's.

Marvin waited till the turtle was facing the front of the tank, then ran quickly down the back wall. The glass was slippery with condensation. As soon as the turtle turned toward him, Marvin froze. Elaine was drifting toward the large rock, and the turtle was now headed that way, stumpy legs churning the water.

Marvin tried to think what to do. The easiest thing would be to crawl onto the rock and pull her out when she floated close enough. But there wasn't time. The turtle was swimming straight for her.

"Elaine," he cried, "when I grab your leg, hold tight!"

Taking a deep breath, Marvin dove off the wall directly into the cloudy green water.

Immediately he was submerged. As soon as he opened his eyes he could see the turtle's massive underbelly above him, his legs thrashing toward Elaine, who was caught in the propulsion, spinning wildly.

Marvin shot up toward Elaine's black shell, reaching blindly for her leg. He sensed rather than saw the snapping jaws of the turtle just as he yanked Elaine away with him into the depths.

They dove, down, down, through the dark water, with Marvin zigging and zagging just out of reach of the turtle. Marvin swam as fast as he could, but minus his peanut-shell float and with one leg gripping Elaine, he had neither the strength nor the speed that he was used to. Every time he glanced behind him, the turtle's head loomed closer, his beady eyes fixed on the two beetles.

Finally they reached the rock. Marvin heaved Elaine over the edge of it and gasped for breath, then immediately swam away, hoping the turtle would follow him instead.

They had no hope of escaping together; it would take too long to climb out of reach.

Fortunately, the turtle swerved after Marvin, who zoomed to the opposite end of the tank. Rushing directly to the corner, Marvin lifted two legs out of the water and frantically tried to pull himself up.

But the glass was too slippery. He crashed back into the pool just as the turtle descended on him with jaws snapping.

"Marvin!" Elaine screamed.

Marvin ducked under the turtle's open mouth and hurled himself at the neck. He grabbed tight with all six legs. The turtle swung his head back and forth, twisting and writhing. Marvin clung tighter. Then the turtle spun back toward the rock, gliding swiftly through the water.

"Marvin!" Elaine cried again. "Jump off!"

Marvin knew that he wouldn't be able to hold his breath much longer. As soon as the turtle neared the rock, he loosened his hold on the muscular neck. He saw Elaine's blurry shape through the water, crouched at the edge of the rock. He flung himself toward her. For a second, the heaviness of the water seemed to trap him. But then Elaine grabbed him, yanking him up, up, up into the clean air.

"Hurry!" she cried. Together they dashed for the slippery back wall of the tank. They could hear the turtle splashing out of the water and lumbering over the rock toward them.

"Don't look back," Marvin warned Elaine, pulling her with him onto the wall. Frantically they scrambled up the glass.

Seconds later, they climbed onto the top rim of the aquarium, well out of reach. They toppled over the edge and half-slid, half-fell to safety.

"Oh, Marvin!" Elaine let out a long breath as they flopped on the ground. "That was a close one! I think I saved your life back there."

"Saved MY life?"

"When I pulled you up on the rock."

"What about when you fell into the tank?" Marvin demanded.

"Oh, I know! Talk about scary. Who would have thought that old turtle would be so fast? We'll have to be more careful next time."

"Next time?" Marvin stared at her.

"You know what I mean," Elaine said dismissively. "Come on, let's go. It's noon already."

They ran across the aquarium table toward the windows, where the long planter filled with herbs beckoned in the sunlight. Marvin could smell the sharp scent of mint, and glimpsed Mama in the distance, untying the yellow hamper and spreading the picnic fare on a fallen basil leaf. He and Elaine hurried past waving fronds of oregano and dill toward their parents.

"There you are," Mama said. "I was

beginning to worry."

Uncle Albert smiled at them. "I told her, 'What trouble can they possibly get into with a bunch of plants? There aren't any humans around.' "

Marvin and Elaine exchanged sheepish glances.

"Sorry," Marvin said.

"We were having so much fun, we didn't notice the time," Elaine added brightly.

"Oh, that's all right," Mama replied. "That was the whole point of coming here today, so you two could relax. Especially you, Marvin."

Marvin secretly made a face at Elaine, but she only shrugged.

"I'm starved," Papa declared. "Let's eat!"

And with that, the six beetles gathered around the bountiful spread — a midday feast of shattered pretzel pieces, blueberries, cantaloupe seeds, muffin crumbs, a semi-sweet chocolate chip, and a fresh oregano salad — and enjoyed their picnic in the shade of the fragrant herbs.

JAMES'S PROBLEM

For the past two days, Marvin had worried about what to do on Wednesday afternoon. Mama and Papa had made their position clear: There were to be no more trips to the Met, and no more drawings.

"It's James's problem now," Papa said. "He's a bright boy. He'll figure out something."

"I know this is important to you, darling," Mama added soothingly, "but you can't take the risk. It affects all of us."

Marvin said nothing, quietly fretting and hoping that some brilliant solution would occur to him before Karl came at four o'clock on Wednesday.

By three o'clock on Wednesday, no such solution had appeared, and Marvin hadn't even seen James since Monday.

"I want to go to James's room," Marvin told his parents. "Even if I can't help him, I have to see what's going to happen!"

Mama and Papa looked doubtfully at each other.

Papa said, "I don't think that's a good idea, Marvin. It will only make this harder for you."

"But what about James? He won't understand. He thinks I'm coming."

Mama shook her head. "Marvin, darling, there's no way to explain this to James. Your father is right. He'll have to figure it out on his own."

"Mama, please!" Marvin felt like crying. All he could think of was James, excitedly getting ready for the Met, sure that Marvin would be right there alongside him.

"I can't just not show up," he pleaded.

Mama sighed.

"Mama, we're friends."

His mother looked at him for a long minute. "All right," she said finally, "but I'm coming with you."

Together they left the cupboard and darted along the kitchen baseboard. William was strapped in a bouncing canvas sling in

179

the doorway, careening madly from one side of the door frame to the other, his feet intermittently thumping the ground.

"Watch out," Mama warned as they skirted treacherously close to his fat flailing legs.

"Ayeeeee!" squealed William. A long string of saliva dangled from his chin.

As they hurried down the hall, they heard voices in the living room.

Mrs. Pompaday sounded annoyed. "Of course he isn't ready. You said four, Karl. That's what we planned on."

James called nervously from his bedroom, "It's okay, Dad. I just need a few more minutes."

Marvin looked at his mother. Karl was here already? James must be in a panic.

"No problem," Karl said sheepishly. "I didn't mean to interrupt anything. I finished early today, and I thought if we got to the Met earlier, that would give James more time."

"More time for what?" Mrs. Pompaday demanded. "Isn't the art lesson at four-thirty? That's what you said."

"Yes, that's right," Karl said easily. "It's not a big deal. I'm ready whenever you are, James."

Marvin and his mother crawled under James's closed door and waited at the edge of his rug, hidden by the cotton fringe. The boy was hunched over his desk, his head in his hands. They could hear him talking to himself, his voice muffled.

"Oh, where are you? Where are you, little guy?" His shoulders shook. "I haven't seen you in *days!* What am I going to do if you don't come?"

Marvin looked at his mother, horrified. "Mama, he's *crying.*"

Mama frowned. "Well, I'm sure he's upset. But he'll pull himself together, you'll see."

"James? Almost ready?" Karl's voice echoed distantly from the living room.

181

James looked around, his eyes wet, his cheeks flushed. He wiped his nose furiously with the back of his hand. "Yeah, Dad, um . . . just a sec."

He stood up slowly and lifted his jacket from the closet doorknob.

"I don't get it," he mumbled, biting his

lip. "Why didn't you come back?"

"Mama," Marvin cried, "he can't do this by himself!"

Mama shook her head firmly. "Marvin, we already discussed this."

"But James is my friend."

"Darling, he's a human! He can't be your friend. You come from different worlds. Why, you can't even communicate with each other."

"But we can, Mama! We do! Not by talking . . . but in other ways. And besides, that's not the only thing that matters." Marvin groaned in frustration. Why didn't Mama understand? The most important things in a friendship didn't have to be said out loud.

James put on his jacket and gazed forlornly around the room. "I know you'd be here if you could," he whispered into the air. "I hope nothing happened to you."

"Mama!" Marvin was beside himself. "Look at him!"

The boy picked up his ink set, turning the navy blue pen case over in his hand. Marvin could see the three gold letters on the top. "I can't draw, not the way you can. I can't do it by myself."

Marvin pictured James alone in Christina's office, faced with the blank paper and the tiny, perfect Dürer drawing. He looked hard at James, at his pale, worried face, the sad slump of his shoulders. He thought back to the disastrous birthday party on Saturday, the loud, indifferent boys, the scolding Mrs. Pompaday who always seemed vaguely irritated by her son.

People like James weren't treated right by the world, Marvin decided. The quiet ones never were. They were doomed to be jostled, bullied, and overlooked because they didn't know how to take up space for themselves, to insist on their own share.

And now James was about to lose the one thing that had finally given him the attention he deserved.

No, thought Marvin. He stared at the boy, sending every ounce of his affection and loyalty pulsing through the air between them. *You're not alone,* he thought. *You have me!*

As soon as he thought it, Marvin knew it was true. He turned to Mama, suddenly determined.

"Mama, he needs me. I can't let him down. You and Papa always tell me to be a good friend."

"Of course we do, darling, but —"

"A good friend is someone you can count on. No matter what."

He watched as James took a breath,

squared his shoulders, and started toward the door.

"I'm going with him, Mama. I have to. He can't do it without me."

"Marvin!" Mama protested, but Marvin was already scuttling out from under the heavy fringe of the rug. He rushed up the door to the brass knob, where he positioned himself in plain view.

"Oh, darling!" his mother cried.

James stopped in his tracks.

"Hey! YOU'RE HERE!" he yelled.

The door swung open. "For heaven's sake, who are you talking to, James?" Mrs. Pompaday demanded.

James gingerly reached for the knob, his hand almost touching Marvin. Marvin climbed onto his finger and quickly crawled under the cuff of his jacket.

"Nobody," James mumbled.

"Well, don't do that, dear. It's odd."

Resting his hand on the door frame, Karl winked at James. "Let's go, buddy. Got your ink set?"

"Yeah, Dad, I'm ready."

"Be careful!" Marvin heard his mother call from far below.

He poked his head out from under the knit cuff and waved at her to show he'd heard. He could see James's wide grin as he and his father strode through the apartment to the elevator, then out of the building into the gray winter afternoon.

THE ART OF THE FAKE

When they met Christina in her office, she greeted them in a flush of excitement. "Here you are! I've been thinking about this all day." She gave James's shoulder a quick pat and beamed at him. "I still can't believe my luck in finding you, James."

James smiled shyly, staring at his sneakers.

"Oh, I know," Christina laughed. "I'm embarrassing you. I do that to my nieces all the time."

Karl walked over to her desk. "Are those the girls in the photo?"

"Hmmm? Oh, yes . . . my sister's children, Katie and Eleanor." She looked at the picture, her eyes shining with affection.

Marvin climbed quickly up to James's collar, for a better look at the photo. He liked the relaxed expression on Christina's face, the way her arms curled comfortably around the children. She looked different in the photo — unguarded. He remembered hearing Karl tell James once that it was hard for people to ever know what they really looked like. Reflections in mirrors weren't accurate, Karl said, because when you stared at yourself in a mirror, you subconsciously composed your face in a way that wasn't your natural expression.

Marvin wondered if that was true when

you were with strangers too. Maybe you only looked like your true self with the people you loved. And maybe that was a face you yourself hardly ever got to see, except in photos like this one.

Karl lifted the frame. "The little one looks exactly like you."

Christina smiled. "Doesn't she? And Eleanor is the spitting image of my sister's husband. Have you noticed how that happens sometimes? The genes of the parents seem to sort themselves out, and the children look like one side or the other. I told Lily she saved me the trouble of having children."

Karl tousled James's hair. "Well, it's not so much trouble, really."

"Oh, I didn't mean it that way," Christina said quickly, glancing at James. "Anyway, it's the kind of trouble I'd enjoy."

Christina seemed to turn shy suddenly, bowing her head to focus on a stack of papers on the desk. "Okay. These are from Denny. They're blank manuscript pages, old ones, from the sixteenth century. That's the trick to forgeries. Everything has to date correctly and show the right signs of wear."

Karl frowned. "But I thought you said it didn't need to be an exact copy . . . since you don't have to convince a collector, just some underworld art thief."

"That's right." Christina turned reassuringly to James. "Your drawing will pass for the real thing, James. I'm sure of it. But we don't want anything on the surface to be a dead giveaway."

She gently lifted the pages and set them on the table, removing the parchment overlay. The sheets were yellowed and tattered at the edges, marked by odd discolorations and blemishes. Marvin thought they showed every bit of their five hundred years.

"The best forgers are meticulous about their materials," Christina continued. "They use old paper, taken from books or manuscripts of the time period. They match the historic shades of ink. They 'age' the work with tears and smudges. There's no surer sign of a fake than an image that's too perfect."

Karl nodded. "Anything real has flaws."

"Exactly. And in the art world, oddly enough, the flaws are what show its value."

James looked at the pages on the table. "But what about my pen-and-ink set? It's not old. Can we still use that?"

We, Marvin thought, flexing his front legs. A trill of anticipation coursed through him.

"If the drawing had to pass inspection by an expert, no. But James, you're able to make such delicate lines with that pen of yours! So like Dürer's."

"What about the ink?" Karl asked.

"The ink has to be brown, as it is in the original drawing. I've been working on that for the past couple of days. I have a sample to try. James, we may need you to do the drawing more than once to get it right. Okay?"

James nodded.

"Okay, then." Christina faced the broad wooden table. "Let's set you up here. The museum closes shortly, and then Denny's going to bring you the original *Fortitude.*"

"The real one?" James turned to his father, looking worried.

Karl raised his eyebrows. "Can you do that? Just take it off the wall? There's no alarm system?"

"Not during the day. Just the guards. We move artworks all the time," Christina answered. She twisted a strand of hair, watching James. "What is it, James? Are you nervous?"

Marvin looked at James's pale face. He was biting his lip.

Christina touched his shoulder, and Marvin dove for cover under the jacket collar. "Don't worry," she said reassuringly. "The drawing is protected by glass — you can't hurt it."

I hope not, Marvin thought. He was trembling with excitement. He'd get to see it up close finally, the real drawing!

"Okay," James said in a small voice.

Christina squeezed his arm. "I'll check on Denny," she said. "And fetch the ink."

As soon as she left, James looked at his father. "What if I break it? Or spill ink on it?"

Marvin cringed, thinking how often Mrs. Pompaday cautioned James not to spill.

Karl laughed. "You won't, buddy. It's in a frame, under glass. We'll make sure it's safe."

"But Dad, it's, like . . . a masterpiece, right?"

Karl considered this. "Well, it's not the *Mona Lisa.* It's not the Sistine Chapel."

James looked at his father, puzzled. "What makes those masterpieces, and not this one?"

Marvin felt compelled to crawl out from under James's collar to hear the answer.

"I didn't say that. A masterpiece is a great work of art. It's the best of an artist's work — one of a kind." Karl rubbed his beard. "But sometimes people don't recognize a masterpiece for years and years . . . till long after the artist's death." He hesitated. "It can be hard to say what makes one work

192

stand out from the rest. What makes the *Mona Lisa* so special? On one level, it's just a picture of a woman smiling."

James shrugged. "It *is* just a picture of a woman smiling."

"But on another level, it's so much more," his father said. "It's full of secrets. Is she proud? Sorry? Flirting? In love? Look at it long enough and you might come to your own answer, but it's a painting that can be seen in a hundred different ways." He smiled a little. "By that standard, *Fortitude* could be a masterpiece, I guess . . . a tiny masterpiece."

"Yeah," James said, satisfied. Marvin gulped, wondering how it was going to feel to copy a masterpiece. Or try to copy a masterpiece.

Not long after Karl and James's conversation, Christina appeared with Denny, who was carrying something wrapped in a large white cloth.

Denny's eyes sparkled. "Hello, friends," he greeted them. "And now, what you've been waiting for . . ."

He carefully removed the cloth and set *Fortitude* in the middle of the table.

Marvin inched forward for a better look. He caught his breath.

The lines were as strong and fine and

lovely as he remembered. The girl gripped the lion fearlessly. The lion reared up in her arms.

James's voice was scarcely more than a whisper. "Is it worth a lot of money?"

Christina nodded. "We paid close to seven

hundred thousand dollars for *Justice*. Dürer's *Virtues* date from the early 1500s, which makes them rare and even more valuable than most of the Old Master drawings."

Denny nodded, his fingers lingering on the drawing's frame. "The Getty was very lucky to get this one. The small size. The excellent condition. The detail, which is truly exquisite. More than a thousand Dürer drawings survive, but his *Virtues* are in a class of their own." He paused. "There's a romance to them."

James looked up at him. "What do you mean?"

"Well, Justice, for example. It's a universal ideal. Civilizations depend on it. Wars are fought over it, and people die for it — or the lack of it."

Christina reached for the dusty volume of Dürer prints and thumbed through it quickly. "There's a wonderful Plutarch quote. Do you know who that is, James? Philosopher and historian in ancient Greece." She scanned the pages. "Here: *Justice is the first of virtues, for unsupported by justice, valor is good for nothing; and if all men were just, there would be no need for valor.*"

"What's valor?" asked James.

"Bravery," Karl said. "Courage."

"Or fortitude," Denny added thoughtfully. "So Plutarch is saying: If everyone were fair, you wouldn't need anyone to be brave."

Christina nodded. "The Greeks thought the four cardinal virtues were related to one another. It was impossible to master one without mastering all of them."

Denny smiled. "Now Nietzsche, on the other hand" — he turned to James — "famous German philosopher, thought the opposite. He believed the virtues were incompatible. He said you couldn't be wise and brave, for instance."

Marvin crawled back under the shadow of James's collar to contemplate this. It had been brave to show himself to James at the beginning of this whole adventure, after he had made the drawing. But it hadn't been very wise, probably. He thought of Dürer's four drawings: *Justice, Fortitude, Temperance, Prudence.* If you had to choose one virtue, which would be the most important? Was it better to be wise or brave? Reasonable or fair? Marvin decided that the answer to that question might depend on your situation.

"Are you ready, James?" Denny asked. He raked his fingers through his gray hair and smiled encouragingly.

"I guess," James said. Marvin thought he

didn't sound ready at all. Karl walked around the table to stand next to him, studying the drawing.

"Don't worry, James," Christina said. "It's more important to be relaxed than to make an exact copy. The key to a good forgery is that sense of ease . . . making the lines smooth and fluid, not halting. Do you know what I mean?"

She crouched next to James, and Marvin immediately scooted farther under the collar, remembering the last time she'd caught sight of him. He could smell her mild, soapy scent, and he noticed again how lovely she was, with her smooth cheeks and shining hair.

Denny said softly, "Every drawing tells a story. It talks to you."

Together, they all gazed at *Fortitude.* Clutching the jacket fabric, Marvin noticed the tension in the girl's sturdy body, the way the lion seemed to both lunge and recoil at the same time.

A breathless hush settled over the room. The noise of rush-hour traffic on the street below seemed miles and miles away. Marvin felt as if they'd all been hypnotized.

Finally, Denny spoke. "Dürer's paintings can sometimes seem quite cold," he commented, still transfixed. "But not his drawings. His drawings are full of humanity."

Christina paused. "But there's always something held back. It's almost as if he couldn't bear to expose his tender imagination."

Marvin understood that feeling. It was as though, in his subjects, Dürer saw something unbearably fragile and beautiful, and he had to steel himself to protect it from the heartless world.

After a minute, Christina turned back to James, her voice coaxing and gentle. "All right, James, take as long as you need. We'll check back in an hour or so, okay? Here's the brown ink." She slid a small glass jar across the table and carefully positioned one of the manuscript pages next to it.

"Oh, and let me clean off your pen. We can't have any trace of your old ink on it." She opened the flat case and lifted James's pen from its snug resting spot, motioning Denny toward a bottle of clear fluid on her desk. "Denny, pass me that, will you?"

Christina poured the solution onto a handkerchief and dabbed the metal nib of the fountain pen. Then she placed the pen back in its case, turning to James expectantly. "Okay?"

Karl bent to hug him. "What do you say, buddy? All set?"

"Yes," James answered. This time, Marvin noticed, his voice didn't waver at all.

"Good man," Denny declared.

And with that, the three adults left the room.

More Than a Copy

When they were gone, James immediately tugged back his jacket cuff, looking for Marvin. When he didn't see him, he checked under his collar. "There you are, little guy," he said, relieved. "Do you think you can do it? The real drawing is right here. Look at it." He plucked Marvin from his nylon perch and gingerly lowered him to the table.

Marvin crawled over to the frame, climbing onto the glass of the original. He memorized the way the two figures leaned into each other, the shape they made on the page. He remembered what Karl and Christina had said of his earlier drawing, that the image was too squashed. He would do bet-

ter this time.

"Did you hear what Christina said about that guy Dürer?" James asked. "All that stuff about the way he drew? Maybe that will help you make your picture look more like his, you know?"

He shook the jar of ink, then unscrewed the cap and set it down next to the blank paper. Inside was a glossy, mud-colored puddle, shot through with glints of reddish gold.

Marvin took a deep breath. He crept to the edge of the cap. He plunged his front legs into the ink, then slowly backed over to the manuscript page and began to draw.

It felt as if time stopped. Marvin was so

focused on the work that he lost a sense of everything around him, including James. The walls of the room seemed to disappear. The table floated away. There was only the page and the ink and *Fortitude.*

He worked quickly, making fluid, delicate strokes. The girl took shape before him, with her strong back, her muscular arms. The lion collided with her in a sinewy, angry mass.

Marvin moved back and forth between the original and his own drawing, checking proportions and scrutinizing the smallest details: the lace trim of the girl's gown, the plume of the lion's tail. The center of the paper blossomed in a dense cross-hatching of fine brown lines.

James said nothing, watching wide-eyed from inches away.

Marvin drew and drew. His eyes burned from concentrating on the drawing, his legs ached.

"It's been an hour," James whispered at one point. "They'll be back soon."

Finally, exhausted, Marvin wiped off his front feet and collapsed on the edge of the paper to survey his work.

"Oh!" James gasped.

His face split in a huge, wondering grin.

"You did it."

Marvin looked at his drawing. It was tiny and beautiful, bursting with energy and life. In every contour, in the least of its details, it *was Fortitude.*

He knew in his heart that he could do no better. He hoped it would be good enough.

There was a quiet knock at the door. "James?" They heard Christina in the hallway. James looked questioningly at Marvin. Marvin ran across the table and onto James's wrist, ducking under his sleeve.

"I'm — um, I'm finished," James called.

Christina, Denny, and Karl filed slowly

into the room.

They walked silently to the table and surrounded James, staring at Marvin's drawing. For a moment, the room was so still it seemed frozen.

Christina spoke first. "Do you know what Dürer said?" she asked, and Marvin could hear the emotion in her voice. *"The treasure secretly gathered in your heart will become evident through your creative work."* She paused. "This drawing is beautiful, James. It's more than a copy. You've made it Dürer's, but also your own."

Beneath the jacket cuff, Marvin shuddered with joy.

"It's amazing," Denny said, shaking his head. "Truly amazing. I wouldn't have believed it possible if I hadn't seen it with my own eyes."

"Do you hear that, buddy?" Karl threw back his head and laughed, as if happiness were bubbling up inside of him and forcing its way out. "You're wowing the experts now. I'd call *this* a masterpiece."

James blushed a deep, bright pink, biting his lip. He turned to Christina. "Do you think other people will believe it's the real thing?" he asked.

"I don't *think* so," Christina said firmly. "I *know* so."

"So what do we do now?" Karl asked.

"You don't do anything," Christina said, smiling at him. "But I have a great deal to do. I have to arrange for a burglary."

Karl's eyes twinkled at James. "Something tells me a masterpiece is about to be stolen."

THE FIGHT

Christina said it would take at least a week to work out the details of the burglary. She'd cleared her plans with the museum's director, the FBI's stolen-art unit, and the New York City police — "That took some convincing, I can tell you," she said — but there were still certain details to be resolved. Denny was working on getting clearance from the Getty, even though the real *Fortitude* wouldn't be at risk.

"Nothing will happen until next week at the earliest," Christina told James as he and Karl prepared to leave. Marvin looked longingly at his finished drawing. What if he never saw it again?

James appeared to be thinking the same thing. He turned to Karl and tugged his father's shirt. "What if something goes wrong and we never get it back?" he asked.

Karl looked at Christina. "Well . . ."

"There's always that danger," she said soberly. She crouched next to James and took his hand. Her slender fingers were so close to Marvin that he could have reached out to touch one. Christina had beautiful hands, he thought: graceful but competent, the kind that seemed equally capable of painting a picture or wielding a hammer.

"I'm sorry, James. I wish I could promise that your drawing will be safe, but I can't."

James was quiet for a minute. "Then I want to come back and see it one more time," he said finally.

Marvin felt a wave of relief. Maybe he wouldn't have to say good-bye to *Fortitude* just yet. Denny looked at James in surprise, but Christina nodded understandingly.

"Of course. It will be here in my office till next week. Why don't you come on Thursday or Friday?"

"Can we, Dad? Please?"

Karl hesitated. "I'll have to ask your mother, James. It's fine with me, but I don't know what her plans are."

James bit his lip anxiously. "I hope we can come."

When they returned to the Pompadays' apartment, Mr. Pompaday swung open the door before they could even knock.

"Karl," he said stiffly, nodding, then beckoned James inside. "Your mother's waiting for you. She has something to tell you." His voice crackled with excitement, which was such an unusual tone for Mr. Pompaday that Marvin emerged from James's coat sleeve, wondering what could possibly have happened.

"Oh," James said, looking confused. "Dad wanted to ask her —"

Karl shook his head at James slightly. "Another time, buddy. I'll call her tomorrow." He bent, and pulled James against him, kissing him warmly. "You did a great job today. A great job!"

"Thanks," James said shyly.

Karl took the pen case out from under his arm and lifted the lid. "I'll just clean off that brown ink for you —" He unseated the pen from its nesting place and stopped.

Marvin froze. There was no brown ink on the pen, of course. The pen had never been dipped in Christina's jar of ink.

Why hadn't they thought of that? Marvin

208

groaned inside. It would have been so easy to do. Instead, the silver nib was shiningly free of ink, from Christina's meticulous cleaning hours earlier.

"Um, that's okay," James said quickly, grabbing the pen from Karl. "I already cleaned it off."

Karl looked at him strangely. "But how —"

"When we were at the museum," James said. He shoved the pen back in the box and slapped down the lid.

Mr. Pompaday muttered impatiently, "Well, if that's it, Karl, we'll say good night. James's mother —"

"Sure," Karl said, studying James with a questioning expression on his face. "I'll talk to you tomorrow, James." He started to back away, then said quietly, "Love you, buddy."

"I love you, too, Dad," James answered, not looking up.

Mr. Pompaday closed the door with a thud and herded James toward the living room. There, in the soft glow of the lamplight, Mrs. Pompaday was perched on a chair near the mahogany card table, with Marvin's first drawing — the little street scene — carefully positioned in front of her.

"Oh, finally you're back!" she cried, clapping her hands like cymbals. "James, the most wonderful thing! I invited the Mortons over today to see your cunning little drawing, and what do you think? They want to BUY it!"

James's eyes widened. "Really?" he asked.

She rushed forward and grabbed James's arm, pulling him to the table. "How much do you think they'll pay, James? How much?"

But you won't sell it, right? Marvin thought. *I made that for you.*

James stared at the drawing. "They'll pay money for it?"

"I did tell them I'd have to check with you. But James, this could be your first sale as an artist! A real artist! Think of that."

"You'll be making more than that father of yours in no time," Mr. Pompaday added, chuckling. "Never thought of art as a lucrative profession, myself, but you just may be onto something with these little pictures of yours."

Marvin crept forward, trying to see James's face. *It was a birthday present,* he thought.

James blushed, his eyes reflecting his parents' eager joy. "How much?" he asked.

"Oh, I want you to guess!" his mother crowed. "No, never mind, you'll never be able to guess. It's too much. . . . FOUR

THOUSAND DOLLARS."

She clapped her hands again at James's shocked expression. "I know, I know! I would never have put such a price on it myself, but it turns out they've been looking for a miniature for their downstairs powder room, and this is perfect."

For their powder room? Marvin turned to James in disbelief. *Say no,* he thought. *Say you won't sell it.*

But James smiled — a wide, slow smile of amazement — and said, "Four thousand dollars! That's awesome! Nobody at school will ever believe it!"

"Then I'll tell them yes?" When James nodded, Mrs. Pompaday snatched him against her in a bracelet-jangling hug. "Oh, James! I'm so proud of you. Look what you've made of yourself."

Marvin inched back under James's jacket cuff in disgust. Humans! Money was the only thing that mattered to them. Not beauty. Not friendship.

Through the dense fabric, he could hear the Pompadays' muffled voices: Mr. Pompaday still chortling over the Mortons' offer, Mrs. Pompaday now urging James to take off his jacket and come into the kitchen for supper.

"I have to put my stuff away," James said.

He walked down the hall to his bedroom, closing the door behind him. Immediately, he peeled off his jacket and searched his arm for Marvin.

Marvin couldn't bear to look at him. As soon as James lifted his wrist, Marvin crawled to the underside. When James turned his arm over, Marvin crawled to the other side again, out of sight.

"What's wrong with you?" James asked. "Do you want to get down?" He rested his hand on the desktop, and Marvin immediately scurried across it, heading toward the wall.

"Hey! Where are you going, little guy?" James dropped his hand in front of Marvin, blocking the way. "Do you need to go home? I can take you, like I did last time. It'll be much faster. Climb up."

Furious, Marvin veered around the boy's outstretched palm and continued toward the wall. He wanted nothing to do with James.

"What is it?" James persisted. "What's the matter?" This time he settled his hand gently over Marvin and scooped him up, bringing him close to his face. He looked at him with troubled gray eyes.

By now, Marvin was seething, not just at James's heartless sale of his drawing, but at

the indignity of being so easily thwarted
when he was trying to leave in a huff. He
turned his rear end toward James, gathered
his legs beneath him, and sank into a small
immobile black mound. (This play-dead
maneuver was a common beetle strategy in
the face of imminent danger. Marvin had

never used it before to show his anger, but he was beginning to realize that communication with humans required a large measure of creativity.)

"You're mad at me," James said.

Marvin didn't move.

"But why?" James seemed genuinely bewildered. "Everything was fine at the museum. You were so great. You were amazing. The way you copied that drawing . . . you're like a genius beetle, do you know that?"

Marvin was determined not to respond.

"What's the matter?" James coaxed. He was quiet for a minute. "It's your street drawing, isn't it? You don't want me to sell it." He let out a long breath and flopped into the chair at his desk. "I don't want to sell it either," he said softly.

Marvin remained in his tight huddle, trying not to listen.

"You know that, right?" James persisted. "I love that picture you made for me. That was my best birthday present ever." He sighed. "It's just . . . You probably can't understand this, but my mom — she's . . ."

James set Marvin down on the desktop, lightly rolling him off his palm. "You can go if you want. I didn't mean to stop you."

Marvin slowly uncurled his legs, but stayed where he was.

James kept talking. "The thing is, she's so proud of me, you know? That's not how she is, usually. And it's not even for something I did — it's for something you did." He crossed his arms on the desk and rested his head on them, his pale face close to Marvin, his breath warm and slightly salty. "It's like this is a special trick she can show off to her friends. I wish" — he hesitated — "I wish she'd be proud of me for regular reasons . . . you know?"

Marvin turned to face him. He thought of Mama and Papa, who were always ridiculously proud of him, even for things that didn't warrant it. It was like being followed around by your own personal cheering sec-tion. Sometimes it bothered him, but mostly it was pretty nice to know that his parents wholeheartedly believed he could do anything, yet were still bursting with pride when he did. He wondered if James had ever felt that way.

James kept talking, his voice husky and low. "They said it wasn't my fault they got divorced. They said that over and over. *It's not your fault, we still love you, you're the most important thing to us.* But if I was the most important thing, how come I wasn't important enough for them to stay together?"

He watched Marvin and waited, as if he thought Marvin might really know the answer. Finally he said, "Because if they'd ever asked me, 'What do you want?' that's what I would have said: all of us together."

Marvin crawled to the edge of James's elbow and looked up at him, not feeling angry anymore.

He sighed. He saw that he would have to forgive James for the drawing. There were too many other things between them.

James let out another long breath. "But you know what? If they hadn't gotten divorced, there'd be no William. So William was the one good thing that came out of it."

Marvin recoiled in surprise. The beetles

all thought William was quite horrible — grabby, irrational, and dangerous. He knew that James didn't feel that way, but he hadn't ever imagined that James would see William as a blessing. However shocking, it was somehow comforting to hear that the pesky baby had brought a spark of pleasure to James's life.

James sat up and rubbed his face. "I don't know why I'm telling you this," he said sheepishly. "I just like talking to you, I guess." He grinned. "And I know you won't tell anyone."

He stretched out his hand again. "Come on, I'll take you home."

Marvin climbed onto the boy's finger, and James headed for the kitchen.

That night, after the fuss over his return, a full report of what had happened at the museum, and a stern scolding from Mama about the risks he'd taken when he disobeyed her, Marvin lay in his bed thinking about what James had said. Eventually, he called to his mother.

"What is it, darling? Your father and I are about to go foraging."

"I can't sleep," Marvin said.

"Well, I'm not surprised. You're completely off schedule from living on human time these past few days. But you must be exhausted from your outing. . . . What's the matter?"

"I don't know. I was thinking about something James said."

Mama sat on the edge of the cotton ball and stroked his shell. "What?" she asked.

"About his parents getting divorced." Marvin thought back to the conversation in James's bedroom. "Why don't beetles ever get divorced?"

His mother considered that for a moment. "Well, our lives are short, darling. What would be the point? We have so little time, we must spend it as happily as possible."

She tucked the cotton fluff more securely around Marvin. "And we expect a lot less than people do. If we get through the day without being stepped on, with a little food to fill our bellies, a safe place to bed down for a few hours, and our family and friends close by — well, that's a good day, isn't it? In fact, a perfect day. Who could ask for more?"

Marvin snuggled into the soft bedding and nodded sleepily. "I guess," he said.

"Also, we have no lawyers," his mother added, leaving the room.

A PERFECT CRIME

The following week passed uneventfully. Mama and Papa were thrilled to have Marvin safe at home again. Elaine was delighted to be regaled with more tales of the outside world. The Pompadays, still gloating over the sale of James's drawing, were busy with their usual activities, though briefly inconvenienced when the timer on the microwave stopped working. Fortunately, Uncle Albert was able to maneuver his way through the vents at the back of the oven and reconnect a loose wire. This fixed the problem, though not before the Pompadays had a heated exchange about unreliable foreign appliances, Mr. Pompaday's lack of handiness, and the fact that if Mrs. Pompaday were a real cook, she wouldn't be using a microwave anyway. Their argument ended abruptly when the microwave's clock started blinking again and Albert slipped triumphantly out the back. (Mrs. Pompaday: "Oh! Look, it's working now." Mr. Pompaday: "See, I fixed it.")

James himself seemed noticeably more cheerful and confident. Marvin spent nearly every afternoon in his bedroom, and he couldn't decide what accounted for the change: the success of copying *Fortitude*? the attention from Mrs. Pompaday over his new talent? the excitement of the pending burglary? Whatever it was, James was happy, which made Marvin happy.

When Friday came, Karl and James, with Marvin in tow, arrived at Christina's office at exactly five-thirty, as she had instructed. Mama and Papa hadn't even put up a fuss about Marvin leaving the apartment this time, since Marvin had spent most of the intervening week extolling the importance of seeing his beloved drawing again for what might be the last time. The burglary had been arranged for that evening, and now that plans were in place, everything seemed to be proceeding very quickly.

Christina greeted them warmly, her eyes

bright. When she saw James, she swooped down and hugged him. He looked startled, but Marvin could tell he was pleased. "How's my favorite forger?" she asked, smiling.

"Okay," he said.

"Ready for a last look at your drawing? It's hanging in the gallery now, right where the original was, and nobody has suspected a thing! Denny helped me make the switch last night. Imagine that, James: All day long people have been staring at a James Terik miniature, thinking it's a Dürer."

James grinned. "Really?"

"Really! When you look at the two drawings side by side, the resemblance is uncanny. And the matting and framing are identical to the original. Denny and I were working on that all day yesterday."

"What about the tracking device?" Karl asked.

"The FBI will handle it," Christina said. "But they explained it to us yesterday. Their agent is going to embed a microchip in the matting before he leaves the building."

"And it won't set off any kind of alarm?" Karl asked. "When the drawing is taken from the museum?"

Christina shook her head. "The microchip can be detected only by the FBI's tracking equipment, not a regular security system. And we don't search visitors exiting the museum. So there shouldn't be a problem. With the tracking unit, the FBI will be able to follow the drawing through the city, until —"

"Until it leads you to the thieves," Karl finished for her.

"Yes! And hopefully, the other stolen drawings."

Karl rubbed his beard. "What if the thief takes just the drawing, not the matting? Then you'd lose the tracking device."

Christina pursed her lips. "I know. We discussed that at length. It's one reason we didn't put the device on any part of the frame. Even if the FBI agent took the drawing as it is, it seems likely the next guy would get rid of the frame for easier transport." She pushed her glasses up more firmly to the bridge of her nose. "But we didn't really have a choice. The microchip would be visible if we put it anywhere on the drawing, because the paper is so old and fragile. If we put it on the matting — well, we all feel more confident the thieves won't see it." She looked at Karl soberly. "But you're right, it's a risk."

Marvin could see that James looked worried, and he was beginning to feel a gnawing pit in his own stomach. "Where's the real drawing?" James asked.

Christina smiled. "It was here in my office last night. I can't tell you how many times Denny and I compared the two, to make sure everything looked exactly right. Then we wrapped up the Dürer and sent it to the vault in the director's office for safekeeping."

"And what about the FBI guy who's going to take James's drawing?" Karl asked. "Is he here yet?"

Christina glanced at her closed office door. "No, not yet. It's been a crazy day. I've been so busy with the FBI, I just got back here a little while ago. I'm not supposed to discuss the details. . . ." She looked at them apologetically for a moment, then capitulated. "Oh, how can I not tell you two, when you're the ones who've made it all possible?"

She took James's hand and pulled him closer, lowering her voice. "No one can know anything about this. Do you understand, James? This whole thing depends on the public — and the underground art world — believing that the real Dürer has been stolen."

Karl, James, and Marvin all watched her intently, waiting for her to go on.

Christina hesitated. "So here's the plan: Tonight we're open late, till nine o'clock. About fifteen minutes before closing, the guards will clear the galleries. Our contact from the FBI stolen-art unit has a Met guard uniform. He'll come into the gallery with a canvas bag after the public has left."

"But don't the other guards know one another?" Karl asked. "Won't they be surprised if they don't recognize him?"

Christina shook her head. "Not on a Friday. On weekends and evenings, we have several fill-in security staff, so that part should be fine."

"And then he'll just take the picture?" James asked. "Right off the wall?" Marvin felt a strange twinge of foreboding.

Christina nodded. "He'll have to make sure no one is watching, and he'll have to move quickly. The idea is that he'll slip the drawing into the bag and go immediately to the left-hand supply closet in the gift shop. . . . You've seen the little gift shop on the second floor, just outside the drawings exhibit? We've left that closet unlocked for him."

"But why?" James asked. "If he's got the drawing, why can't he just leave with it?"

"Let her finish, James," Karl said gently. He turned to Christina. "I'm assuming nobody can walk through the checkpoints carrying a large bag, even a security guard."

"It's safer not to risk that," she agreed. "So we'll have a change of clothes for him in the closet, including a suit jacket with an inside pouch — you know, flat, reinforced, waterproof — that is the right size to hold *Fortitude.* He'll also find the tools he needs to remove it from the framing material and to install the microchip in the matting. He'll change into regular clothes, put the drawing in the inside jacket pocket, leave the supply closet when he's sure the hallway is empty, and exit with the rest of the crowds as the museum is closing."

From beneath James's cuff, Marvin could see Christina's pleased expression, as if the entire plan had been executed flawlessly in the few moments she took to describe it.

"Wow," James said.

Karl nodded thoughtfully. "It's the perfect crime. You seem to have thought of everything."

Christina frowned slightly. "Well, I'd better have thought of everything. There's a lot at stake. He'll only have about fifteen minutes to accomplish all this without arousing suspicion and without another guard noticing the drawing is missing. But if everything goes smoothly, it should work."

James rocked nervously back and forth on his sneakers, and Marvin clung to his jacket for dear life. "Can I see it now? My drawing?"

Christina looked at her watch. "Oh, I wanted to go with you! I haven't had a chance to get to the gallery all day. But I can't now, unfortunately. Denny and I have to review everything one more time with the FBI agent. Go and have a good look . . . and James?" She rested her hand on his head and smiled at him. "Don't worry. This isn't the last time you'll see your wonderful drawing. I'm sure of it."

James looked up at her suddenly. "What about you? Will we see you again?" he asked.

Startled, Marvin turned to Christina. James had a point, he realized. All the preparations for the fake burglary were finished now, so there would be no further reason to meet with Christina . . . not until Marvin's drawing was recovered. If it was recovered.

"Sure we will, buddy," Karl said quickly, sounding embarrassed. "You'll let us know what happens, right, Christina?"

"Oh, of course I will!" Christina swept a strand of hair off her forehead and tucked it firmly behind her ear, as though all the challenges they faced would be resolved as easily. "I couldn't have done any of this without you. Hopefully I'll have something to report this weekend." She smiled at them ruefully. "But I have to tell you, these FBI people are not very forthcoming. They won't include me in anything! I can't see their tracking equipment; I can't be with them while they monitor what's happening to the drawing."

Karl laughed at her. "Well, that's not surprising. We're talking about the FBI, after all. It's their job to be secretive."

"Yes, I suppose so. And at least they've promised to give me updates over the weekend. Who knows? Maybe before too long, I'll have the pleasure of introducing you to *Justice* herself." Christina beamed at them, then hurriedly ushered them out of her office.

"We can't stay long, buddy, okay?" Karl said as they walked down the long hall and through the hidden door into the drawings gallery. "I promised your mom I'd have you back by seven, and it's after six already."

"Okay," James agreed. "I just want to see it, that's all."

In the distance, where the gallery opened onto the second-floor stairwell, Marvin could see the airy marble hall, flanked by

227

statues and softly lit display cases of vases and bowls. A crush of people in winter coats poured through the gallery entrance.

Karl's hand landed on James's shoulder. "This way," he said, and then, crouching next to James and pointing across the room: "Look!"

And there, right where the original had hung, was *Fortitude,* the girl's curved arms sturdily clasping the lion. Marvin felt a swell of pride. He held the edge of James's cuff, straining for a better view.

James reached for his father's hand, tugging him toward the drawing. "It's hanging there with all the real ones!" he whispered.

"Well, it sure looks like it belongs." Karl grinned. "You're the master."

They threaded their way through the crowd toward the wall, then patiently waited for an older couple to step aside.

"Okay, two minutes, buddy," Karl said softly.

James nodded, staring at the drawing. Marvin wanted to climb higher for a better look, but there were so many people around he didn't dare. Just as he was growing frustrated with his angled, partially obscured view, James raised his arm to his shoulder, pretending to scratch the side of his neck. Grateful, Marvin quickly crawled from

jacket sleeve to collar. Now he was almost eye level with the drawing.

He took a deep, happy breath and gazed at his work.

And then his heart stopped.

This wasn't his drawing.

It was Dürer's.

Dürer's! Marvin could tell instantly. But all he felt was confusion. Had he misunderstood? Had they not switched the drawings yet?

He was certain that he was looking at the original. As faithfully as he had followed Dürer's lines, as carefully and reverently as he'd copied each whorl of hair and bulge of sinew, Marvin knew that the intricate

strokes in the artwork before him weren't
his. A drawing was as personal as handwrit-
ing. Yours might look similar to someone
else's — even identical in the eyes of a
stranger — but you could always recognize
your own.

Marvin crawled out from under James's

collar. He was fully exposed to the light and air, directly in the sightlines of the surrounding museum-goers, but he couldn't help himself. This was the original, as dignified and melancholy and fully Dürer's as it had ever been.

His mind raced. Why was the Dürer drawing hanging here instead of the copy? Where was his own drawing? He gripped James's jacket, trying to piece together what could have happened. Christina had said the real drawing was in the museum director's office, in a vault. How could this be? Marvin felt a growing sense of dread.

He began to run back and forth along the edge of James's collar, frantic. The FBI agent was coming to take this drawing, in nearly two hours' time. What if Christina had made a mistake? What if she'd somehow mixed up the two pictures?

There was a tracking device, Marvin reminded himself, trying to calm down. The FBI would be monitoring that. But now he had to consider the possibility that the tracking device was about to be affixed to the Dürer original by mistake. And suddenly, Christina's warnings about the danger of the plan — the chance that the drawing would be truly stolen and lost forever — filled his head like a drumbeat. That had been alarming enough when Marvin believed his own drawing was at risk. But now it looked like the *real* Dürer might be taken from the museum and whisked into that strange, foggy world of art thieves and stolen masterpieces.

Above him, Karl and James seemed not to suspect a thing. "It's fantastic, James," Karl was whispering. "Everything about it looks real."

That's because it IS real! Marvin wanted to shout. He scuttled back into hiding before Karl could see him, awash in panic. How could he tell them? The real Dürer *Fortitude* was about to be stolen, just like the other three *Virtues!*

"Look at the detail," Karl continued. "To see a drawing, really see it, takes time."

Yes! Marvin thought. *Look at it, James. Look at it and you'll know.*

But James only stood quietly before the drawing, gazing at it steadily. Finally, Karl said, "We should go. You'll see it again before too long."

No! Marvin screamed silently.

"I hope so," James said uncertainly. He shifted from one foot to the other, hesitating. *Please, James,* Marvin prayed. *It's not my drawing.*

"Come on, buddy." Karl clasped James's

shoulder.

As James started to turn away, all Marvin could think of was the drawing. He couldn't bear to leave. Not knowing what else to do, he rushed to the tip of James's collar, pointed himself toward the wall, and jumped into the void.

FATE AND *FORTITUDE*

Marvin plummeted headlong through space for several long seconds. *Thump!* He crashed into the floor of the gallery, rolled twice, and came to a halt. Fortunately, the room's low-pile gray carpet softened his landing. He was a little dazed but none the worse for wear. Shoe-clad feet milled around him, and James's blue sneakers were fast disappearing in the distance. He knew it was suicide to linger out in the open. He crawled as fast as he could to the wall and waited near the scuffed baseboard.

Marvin had to make his way to the drawing, but it seemed too risky to climb the wall when so many people were looking at the pictures. He knew that his black shell would be hard to miss once he started the trek across the expanse of wall. Though his stomach clenched over the danger facing Dürer's drawing, he decided there was nothing to do but wait till the gallery cleared out. In the flurry of closing, he hoped he could make his way to *Fortitude* unnoticed, before the FBI agent did.

The evening passed quickly. To take his mind off his fears, Marvin occupied himself with people-watching, which was one of his favorite pastimes anyway. He counted the different types of shoes that strolled past his hiding place: 12 black loafers, 6 brown loafers, 4 stilettos, 8 black lace-up shoes, 6 pumps, 4 hiking boots, 8 dress boots, 11 sneakers (and one cast). He tried to predict how long people would linger in front of the pictures based on their type of shoe. The pumps and black loafers won, with the hiking boots a close second. The sneakers were divided between those who stayed longer than anyone (college students, Marvin decided), and those who rushed off with barely a glance (children).

After a couple hours of this, Marvin was starving. The floor was disappointingly free of litter, probably due to the museum's prohibitions on food and drink. But a few

minutes later, a woman walked by pushing
a stroller, and Marvin was delighted to see
a Cheerio tumble off her toddler's lap. He
studied the movements of the crowd thoroughly before making a mad dash to retrieve
it. Then, just as he and Elaine did at home,
he wedged his head and forelegs through
the hole in the Cheerio, pushed off with his
rear legs, and sent it rolling like a hoop
toward the baseboard, whisking him to
safety. When he reached the edge of the
carpet, he extracted himself and settled
down to dine. The Cheerio was a little stale,
but sweet and crunchy nonetheless: a very
satisfying evening meal.

Finally, the speaker system chimed, and a
woman's voice echoed through the gallery:
"The museum will be closing in fifteen
minutes. Please proceed to the exits now."

Marvin hesitated only a moment, making sure that people were really turning to leave, then scurried up the wall as fast as he could. When he reached the corner of *Fortitude*'s wooden frame, he paused just long enough to look at the drawing, admiring the delicacy of lines that weren't his own. Then he ducked out of sight behind the lower left corner of the frame.

He didn't have long to wait. A moment later, he heard swift footsteps approach the drawing, then felt the picture being lifted from the wall. He held fast as the frame was shoved hastily into some kind of canvas bag, pitch-black inside. Marvin could see nothing but dark fabric all around him. He looked up, and through the narrow opening at the top, he caught sight of thick fingers gripping the handle, the knuckles sparsely covered in hair. The bag swayed and bounced for a few minutes; then, with a gentle thud, it stopped.

This must be the supply closet, Marvin realized. He heard the rustle of cloth and inched up the side of the frame. The darkness of the closet was no impediment to Marvin, who was well used to navigating at night. He could see a short, stocky man moving quickly and confidently, casting aside a navy blue guard uniform.

Suddenly, the frame was snatched from the canvas bag and laid facedown. Marvin had to reposition himself on its side, flattening his body. He'd forgotten this part of Christina's plan. The frame was about to be disassembled. He had to keep out of sight. He heard the *clip, clip* of wire cutters removing the hanging apparatus. A knife flashed above him, perilously close. He shrunk away from the blade that glided expertly through the backing of the picture in a crisp rectangle.

Marvin prayed he wouldn't be knocked off. The next few minutes were critical. If he got bumped or shaken loose — or worse yet, if the man saw him and swatted him away — who could say where *Fortitude* would end up?

He heard the tear of paper. Abruptly, a penlight flashed in the darkness, sending a narrow white beam onto the back of the picture.

Marvin dodged out of sight, terrified. Now he could see the man, his forehead creased in concentration. He had dark hair and an otherwise bland appearance. He could be anyone, Marvin thought — probably an advantage for an undercover FBI agent. The man grunted, tearing off the rest of the backing until Marvin saw the pale matting. Just as the man was about to lift the drawing from the frame, Marvin leapt onto the matting. It felt firm beneath his legs. When he peered over the edge, he saw the yellowed, ancient paper that was surely the reverse of Dürer's masterpiece. He could smell it too — the musty scent of centuries.

Holding the matting gingerly with one hand, the man set down the penlight. Marvin cowered out of sight, watching him remove something tiny and silver from his inside pocket. It must be the microchip, he realized. The man lifted the matting and turned it quickly and expertly, making a small cut with his knife, while Marvin hugged the edge. It was like surgery, Marvin thought, this delicate task of embedding the microchip in the side of the matting, where it wouldn't be seen. After several minutes of manipulation, during which Marvin could hear the man's heavy, impatient breathing, the penlight clicked off.

The microchip was in place.

Marvin barely had time to secure himself against the back of the matting when a piece of something stiff was pressed against his shell. The drawing swung through the air and glided smoothly into a small, tight space.

It must be the jacket pouch, Marvin realized. *Fortitude* was ready for its journey.

It was completely dark inside the jacket, and even Marvin, who was very accustomed to small, dark places, felt a wave of claustrophobia. He remembered the time he and Elaine had gotten stuck in Mrs. Pompaday's eyeglass case when she'd snapped it shut one evening; how he'd panicked and pushed futilely against the felt walls, and Elaine had made fun of him for almost throwing up. Fortunately, Mrs. Pompaday had decided to watch a rerun of one of her shows, and it wasn't long before the case was opened again. (Even more fortunately, she was so absorbed in the television that she didn't notice two shiny black beetles making their escape.)

Now, Marvin felt the jacket sway with the movements of its owner. He could tell when the man left the closet; when he paused to make sure he hadn't been seen; when he strode through the hallway and tripped briskly down the museum's central staircase. Fragments of Cheerio sloshed uncomfortably in Marvin's stomach.

Bouncing along against the man's warm, substantial chest, Marvin could hear the noises of the crowds through the thick cloth. He felt the change in temperature as they exited the Met into a chilly New York evening. A car door opened and slammed shut. The man mumbled an address to someone, then Marvin heard the rapid beeps of a cell phone keypad.

He strained to follow the conversation.

"Yeah, it's done," the man said. "Nope. I'll be there in twenty minutes. What's the room number? Okay, see you then."

This would be the first exchange, Marvin thought, but not the endpoint of the journey for the drawing. It was so hard to remember what was supposed to happen, and yet so important to do so! Marvin hunched fretfully in his spot trying to concentrate, with what seemed like cardboard pressing against him. First, the FBI agent was supposed to give the drawing to an intermediary — wasn't that what Christina had told them? A contact in the underground art world. Then it would be handed off to the real thieves.

The FBI must be tracking the drawing's path, right? Maybe everything would be okay. After all, the plan had been to follow the trail of the fake drawing and ultimately retrieve it. Marvin thought of Christina, of the dangers she'd mentioned, the chance that they'd never see his drawing again. He thought of James and his uncertainty when he looked at the drawing for the last time. Then, suddenly and in a flood of longing, he thought of Mama and Papa. A destination twenty minutes away would still be in the city . . . but what if the drawing was bound for someplace else? And what if Marvin was stuck here, its unwitting companion and helpless protector, unable to escape? He might never see his family again.

The risk he had taken became shockingly clear: His fate and *Fortitude*'s were one and the same. He shuddered, feeling the dull thrum of the car's engine as it made its way through the busy, tired city.

THE MIDDLEMAN

Marvin felt the car stop. The man rustled out and strode a short distance, purposefully and without hesitation. Inside the dark pocket, Marvin tried to guess what was happening. The man had asked for a room number on the phone: Were they now in an office? a hotel? He could tell from the falling sensation in his stomach that they'd boarded an elevator. Then the motion stopped and there were quick steps, followed by a muted knock.

A new voice, muffled but terse, asked, "Do you have it?"

Was this the go-between, ready to ferry the Dürer drawing to the real thieves?

"In here."

"Show it to me."

Marvin had no time to prepare. He tried to stay where he was, frozen, while the drawing was lifted from its protective sleeve. Just as *Fortitude* emerged into the bright light of the room, a lip of fabric caught Marvin's shell and knocked him from his perch. He grasped in vain for the edge of the matting, but missed. He found himself hurtling through the air, landing with a smack on the hard, smooth surface of a laminated table.

Tucking his legs beneath him, Marvin held perfectly still, hoping he hadn't been seen. The wood surface was dark, fortunately. When he peeked around, he saw the bland decor of a hotel room, fully recognizable from all the soap operas he and Elaine had watched on television with Mrs. Pompaday: dark carpeting, floral bedspread, simple, shiny furniture. The FBI agent had set the Dürer drawing in the middle of the table, inches from Marvin. A thin, bearded man leaned over it with a magnifying glass, scrutinizing the details.

For a minute, Marvin felt a jolt of fear. But then he remembered that this was the real drawing, not his forgery. It was sure to pass inspection.

Neither man spoke.

"Okay," the bearded man said finally. "I'll take it to my contact."

"What about my share?" the FBI agent asked.

"There, in the envelope." The bearded man gestured to a flat brown package on the nightstand, which the FBI agent promptly slipped into his suit pocket.

The two men turned toward the door, and Marvin drew a deep breath. Here was his chance. He dashed across the expanse of table in the direction of the drawing. But suddenly he heard a *thump!* A huge hand slapped the surface next to him, sweeping him off the table. He tumbled through the air and landed in a dense woven forest of

green carpeting. It smelled faintly like ciga-
rettes.

A shoe stamped the ground near him,
then stamped again, closer. Marvin raced
for the shelter of the table leg.

Far above him he heard the FBI agent ask,
"What was it?"

"Some kind of beetle," the bearded man answered. "This thing better not be infested with bugs."

"Nah, it's probably from the hotel. Bedbugs."

Bedbugs! Marvin stiffened with indignation. Humans were so ignorant.

The thin man snorted in disgust, then followed the FBI agent to the door.

As Marvin watched the FBI agent leave the room — his last link to the museum and James and safety — he felt truly alone.

THE SECRET JOURNEY

For Marvin, the prospect of spending the night in the hotel room was a grim one, but it quickly became apparent that the bearded man wasn't going anywhere. He made two phone calls with a cell phone. During one, he spoke in a language Marvin didn't understand. During the second, he said: "I have it." Then: "Tomorrow at ten o'clock, where we discussed. Yes, I'll make sure. See you then."

While Marvin concealed himself in the dense carpet beneath the table, the man strode to the closet and removed a black leather satchel. He placed it flat on the floor a few feet from Marvin, unzipping it. Inside were several thick paper folders. After opening one of these, he lifted the drawing carefully from the table and settled it between the leaves of the folder. Then, deftly, he closed the entire bundle and zipped the satchel shut.

Marvin watched all this with mounting apprehension. He had to make his way back to the drawing, but zippers were notoriously beetle-proof.

The man put the satchel back in the hotel closet. He bolted and chained the door, kicked off his shoes, and lay on the bed. A minute later, the TV came on, and Marvin heard the man tear open a plastic wrapper and begin crunching on something. The evening passed uneventfully, with the TV droning, the man snacking, and Marvin lulled into a fitful sleep in his hiding place.

When Marvin opened his eyes, the room was pitch-black, and the man was snoring. Marvin knew he had to figure out a way to get inside the satchel, but he was hungry, and morning was hours away. He crawled laboriously across the thick carpet to the nightstand, where the man was sure to have left the remains of whatever he was eating. And indeed, when Marvin reached the top, he found a crumpled red and yellow wrapper and a pile of hard shells.

Peanut shells, Marvin realized. He felt a pang of longing for his peanut-shell float, lost in the Pompadays' bathroom drain. Oh, how lovely it would be to take a dip in his bottle cap–swimming pool right now! It had only been two weeks since his post-drainpipe bubble bath, but it seemed like centuries ago . . . before he made his first drawing, before he and James became friends, before he knew anything about an artist named Albrecht Dürer.

There was nothing left to eat on the night-stand, but there *was* a half-filled glass of water. Feeling slightly cheered, Marvin tucked a piece of peanut shell under one leg and climbed up the side of the glass. He hesitated a moment on the rim, staring at the placid water below. Then he held his breath and dove, landing with a soft *plop!* A few feet away, the man stirred and rolled over. Marvin pushed the peanut shell in front of him and kicked his legs, swimming in widening circles, with the cool, clean water lapping over his shell. He felt better already.

Sometime later, refreshed from his mid-night swim, Marvin climbed the wet wall of the glass and shook himself off. He found a crumpled tissue near the clock radio and carefully wiped off his shell. Then he

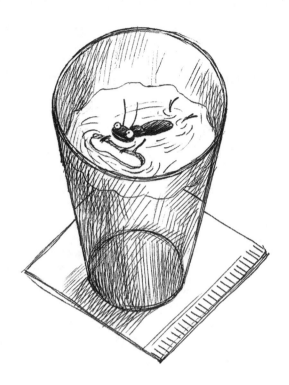

crawled down to the floor, across the rug, and under the closet door, which took a considerable amount of time.

Marvin hesitated at the base of the satchel, trying to decide where best to secure himself. Eventually he chose the flap that covered the outside pocket, wedging himself under the leather buckle. Here, he had both a firm grip and a good vantage point for seeing what was going on.

He must have fallen asleep again, because he awoke jarringly to the bang of the closet door being thrust open and a bright wash of sunlight flooding over him. The thin, bearded man lifted the satchel and set it on the table. He moved about the hotel room quickly, gathering his things, then picked up the satchel again and hurried out of the room.

Minutes later, they were outside on the sidewalk, moving at a brisk pace through a steady stream of people bundled in winter coats and scarves. Marvin shivered under the buckle; it had been much warmer inside the FBI agent's coat. Where were they going now? Another rendezvous. This was a part of the city Marvin had never seen before. Immense buildings shouldering against one another and reaching up, up, up to the sky. Broad avenues crowded with cars and buses. Vast shop windows filled with clothing, jewelry, electronics. After several blocks, they came to a massive gray building with spires — a church, Marvin decided. The man climbed the steps quickly and ducked inside.

The cavernous, shadowy space was crowded with people, some lighting candles, some whispering in small groups, some nestled in the pews, heads bowed in prayer. The thin, bearded man sat near the end of the last pew. Marvin looked quickly around. What now? A few minutes later, another man slid into the pew. Neither one spoke.

The thin, bearded one set the satchel down
next to the other man, stood up, and walked
away.

Marvin held his breath.

Abruptly, the other man grabbed the
handle of the satchel. He picked it up so
quickly and with such force that Marvin lost
hold of the buckle and tumbled into the side
pocket. He could see nothing, but he knew
that the drawing was on the move again. He
tried to scramble up the inside of the pocket

for a better view, but the brisk motion kept knocking him back to the bottom. Eventually, he gave up.

He heard a car door close, then the faint beeps of a telephone and a new voice speaking softly. The man had a thick accent, and Marvin couldn't understand the words. He could feel the rumble of the engine. Where were they going now?

A long time passed, or so it seemed to Marvin, who struggled to guess what was happening in the world beyond his enclosure. There were stops and starts and brief bursts of conversation, or perhaps instruction.

Were they still in New York? Marvin had no way of knowing. In the tense darkness, floating through an unknown, distant world, his mind looped back through time, to James's birthday party, to the night he'd sketched the street scene, to his first breathless glimpse of *Fortitude.* He could feel the presence of the drawing through the leather wall of the satchel. It comforted him somehow. He thought of what Christina had said about Albrecht Dürer: a sad, lonely man, determinedly wielding his pen to bring the girl and the lion to life.

Without meaning to, Marvin drifted off to sleep. He awoke when the motion stopped and the satchel was set down with a thud.

Someone unzipped the satchel and opened it, which meant that the pocket where Marvin was hiding was immediately pressed flat. Marvin crawled quickly to the opening and squeezed out onto a wooden surface. He heard the foreign voice again, this time speaking in halting English.

"Here she is," the man said. "Beautiful, no?"

Another voice responded. "Worth every penny. And now she's almost home."

Marvin's entire body went rigid with shock. He immediately recognized the voice.

HIDDEN *VIRTUES*

Denny!

At first, Marvin was overcome with relief. Denny was here! Now everything would be all right. Surely he would recognize the drawing as Dürer's original. He and Christina must have discovered their mistake. The ruse was over. *Fortitude* would be on its way back to the Met in no time!

"We won't be needing this anymore, will we?" Denny said.

Marvin inched out from under the satchel just in time to see Denny remove *Fortitude* from its matting. They were in what appeared to be the empty lobby of a small building, with glass exit doors on either end, and benches pressed against the walls.

"The cab is waiting for you?" Denny asked the dark-haired man who was hunched over the satchel.

"Sì, signore."

"Go quickly, and leave this on the floor of the cab. That will keep them busy for a while." Denny handed him the piece of matting. "And this is for you." He held out a fat white envelope.

Marvin had no time to puzzle over this exchange because he knew he had only a few seconds to escape. He crawled out from under the satchel and scuttled across the bench to where Denny was sitting. He climbed onto Denny's corduroy trousers and gripped a belt loop with all six legs.

The other man stuffed the bulging envelope into his jacket. "Grazie, signore." Briskly, he shoved the matting back in the satchel, zipped it shut, and hurried through the glass door onto the street.

Denny mumbled to the drawing, "All right, my darling. I have some new packaging for you, and we'll be on our way." He set *Fortitude* gently in a heavy folder, then inside a briefcase.

Marvin shivered, still trying to make sense of what was happening. He felt a twinge of uncertainty. When would they return to the

museum?

Denny stood and his coat flapped over Marvin, obscuring his view. He must have walked out onto the street because it was cold again and they were engulfed in the noise of the city.

This time the motion didn't last long, and it was all walking, Marvin could tell. Eventually, he heard the soft sucking sound of elevator doors and the ding of a button being pressed. A few minutes later, the elevator doors opened and keys jangled.

There was a faint rustling and the sound of Denny humming. Marvin heard him set the briefcase down and unlock it. He must

be removing the drawing now.

"There you are, my beauty," Denny said softly.

He tossed off his coat, and finally Marvin could see. They were in a small, dark room, lit only by a lamp in one corner. It was some kind of study, Marvin decided, paneled in rich, reddish brown wood, with shelves of books lining the walls. Denny had placed the drawing on a large polished table, and when Marvin looked on either side of it, he gasped.

There were three other drawings on the table.

Prudence.

Temperance.

Justice.

"Time to join your sisters," Denny said. "How long we've waited for you!"

AMONG THIEVES

Marvin's head was spinning. What did Denny mean? Here they were: Dürer's four *Virtues*. As confused and scared as he was, he was overcome by a yearning to look at them. It took every ounce of his self-control to stay hidden under the belt loop, silent and still.

All the long-lost, stolen drawings, here with Denny!

The microchip was gone. There was no way for the FBI to find them. Marvin couldn't make sense of it. Had Christina planned the whole theft? Had she switched the two drawings herself?

He trembled with horror. There could be

only one explanation: Denny and Christina had stolen the drawings, all of them. As shocking as it seemed, they must have been working together from the beginning. And this was their goal: to steal the final *Virtue!*

But why?

Denny leaned over the table, and Marvin edged out from under the belt loop to stare at the four drawings. His heart leapt in recognition. The fine, steady pen strokes were like a greeting from an old friend. The women in the other drawings were immediately recognizable as Dürer's: Tiny as the images were, the figures were solid and substantial, anchored to the paper. Their expressions had the same pensiveness that *Fortitude*'s had — a kind of willed loneliness.

In *Prudence,* a maiden shunned the winged cupid who offered her a laurel wreath. In *Temperance,* she poured some kind of liquid from a small jug into a cup. The lines were as delicate and miraculous as the pattern on a butterfly's wing.

Finally, Marvin turned to *Justice.* The drawing had a dense, breathing presence not at all like the flat image in the book Christina had shown them. The girl gazed sadly into the distance, her sword resting at her side, as if she were already resigned to

the unfairness of the world. She raised her
scales like a lantern.

Marvin heard a long sigh. He realized with
a start that he and Denny were caught in
the same reverie, transfixed by the drawings.

Denny straightened and took out his cell
phone. Marvin quickly dropped from his
belt loop to the table, hiding in the grooved

wood at its edge.

"Liesl? It's Denny. How are you, my dear? Yes, still as planned, into Frankfurt. I've purchased an open ticket because I'm not certain what day I'll be traveling. You'll arrange my transportation from the airport?"

Denny paused, listening. "Good. Yes, that's right. I'll be in touch. See you soon, Liesl."

So that was it, Marvin thought. Denny and Christina must be planning to take the drawings out of the country. "Liesl" had a foreign sound to it.

Marvin watched Denny decant a bottle on the desk and pour an amber liquid into a squat crystal glass. He turned to the drawings.

"To Virtue," he whispered huskily, raising the tumbler, and Marvin thought Denny sounded as if he was about to cry. "And to Virtue's master, the astounding Albrecht Dürer."

He drained the glass and set it on the desk. As Marvin watched, he gently concealed the drawings under several sheets of the protective paper, then left the room.

Marvin crawled across the table to where the drawings lay. As he crouched there, wondrously close to them, he was filled with confusion. It was impossible to think of

Denny and Christina as thieves. They were devoted to Dürer's art. Marvin pictured the two of them in Christina's office, interrupting each other with their passion for the drawings. Was it all an act? None of this made sense.

Then he remembered something Denny had said about people who stole works of art: that sometimes, they did it for love.

HATCHING A PLAN

As Marvin huddled there, inches from Dürer's tiny masterpieces, a thin, sharp prick of resolve began to form inside him. He had to do something. But what? There had to be some way to stop this terrible theft. If only James were here! He needed his friend's help now more than ever.

Marvin scurried down the table leg and across the rug to the desk. Swiftly, he climbed up and crossed its smooth expanse to the window ledge. The glass panes were filmy with winter grit, but Marvin could see the length of the street quite clearly. It was a tree-lined block with handsome brick and stone town houses on either side, interspersed with shops and restaurants. Not dissimilar to the Pompadays' own neighborhood, Marvin thought. So perhaps they were still on the Upper East Side somewhere. This notion comforted him, even though a few city blocks would be a month's journey from a beetle's perspective.

He scanned the desk desperately, trying to think what to do next. There was an upright metal tin of pencils and pens, a pad of paper, a small tray of paper clips and rubber bands, and a sheaf of envelopes and newspapers. Marvin crawled over to the stack of papers.

It must be Denny's mail, Marvin thought. He knew a little about the human system of mail, because Papa had explained it to him several weeks ago, when, tragically, Cousin Buford had been scooped up with Mrs. Pompaday's real-estate contracts, sealed inside a flashy orange and purple Federal Express envelope, and mailed to one of her clients. When Marvin asked where he'd been sent to, Papa said that the address was written on the front of the envelope, though the beetles had no way of deciphering it. (Comfortingly, Papa did explain that, wherever Buford was headed, he was sure to arrive by 10:30 the next morning.) The family could only pray he'd survived the journey and made a new life for himself somewhere in the city. Privately, Marvin had his doubts about Buford's ability to make a sandwich, much less a new life for himself. But there was no point in dwelling on what couldn't be helped.

Thus Marvin knew that the writing on the envelope told the mailman where to deliver it. He hesitated at the edge of the stack. One of the newspapers had a white label stuck to it. Could it be the address of this apartment? The place where Dürer's *Virtues* were being held captive? Marvin considered this possibility. If there was some way to get the mailing label to James, he'd at least know where to look for the stolen drawings . . . as long as he got the address before Denny packed up the drawings and left the country.

It was a long shot, but the only idea he had at the moment, and it was certainly better to do *something* than to sit there fretting while the drawings disappeared forever.

He crawled across the thin newsprint to the label. It had to be unstuck somehow. Careful to protect the lines of type, he gently chewed the foul-tasting yellow glue that gummed the label to the paper. Using his legs to lift and tug it, he eventually dislodged the whole thing.

Pleased with himself, Marvin dragged the

label over to an empty surface of the desk. It was slightly tatty at the edges and wet from his chewing, but it still held three complete lines of black letters. He spread it flat and set about meticulously folding and rolling it, exactly as he did with his blanket and towel whenever the beetles went camping. When he'd reduced the label to a tidy bundle that was about as long as he was, he scanned the desktop for something to tie it with.

He caught sight of Denny's jacket, flung over the chair. A scattering of Denny's gray hairs clung to the shoulders, just as Marvin had hoped. He crawled over to fetch one and then used it to tie the rolled label to his underbelly, cinching the strand of hair like a belt.

As one would imagine, this made it very

difficult indeed for Marvin to walk. He
waddled back to the stack of mail and sat
down under the corner of the newspaper,
heaving with exhaustion. Now he just had
to think of a way to get the label in James's
hands.

His thoughts were interrupted moments

later when Denny appeared in the doorway of the study, speaking urgently into his cell phone.

"What? What do you mean? Christina, I don't understand."

Christina! His accomplice. Marvin shuddered with disgust. How had he let himself become so fond of her?

"What happened?" Denny continued. "They did? Just the matting? Oh, of course, with the tracking device. My dear, calm down, it's difficult to understand you."

Marvin scooted out from under the newspaper to hear him better. Why was Christina upset? Their plan had worked perfectly.

"Well, it's a terrible shame, but why are you so —"

There was a long silence, and Denny leaned against the table, listening intently. He rested one hand inches from the drawing of *Justice,* tapping the table lightly. Suddenly he sucked in his breath.

"No! The *real* Dürer? Christina, you must be mistaken."

Marvin scooted out from under the pile of mail, thoroughly bewildered. Of course it was the real Dürer, they'd stolen it themselves. Very faintly, he could hear Christina's high, frantic voice on the other end of the line.

"No, I was in the gallery yesterday, and I didn't notice anything amiss. Of course I wasn't looking closely, since you'd wrapped it up yourself. You're right, it was confusing, but my dear . . . I just can't believe it. Are you sure?" Denny paused.

So Christina hadn't known! So many feelings raced through Marvin that he barely remembered to hide himself when Denny walked toward the desk to get his coat. In the shadow of the newspaper, he slumped in relief. Christina was not involved. Her love for the drawings was real. Her friendship with James and Karl was true.

"Yes, yes, I'll come over at once," Denny said. "I need to see this for myself." Marvin could hear another flood of tinny commentary through the phone, and Denny waited, one hand on his coat.

"It's too much to contemplate, that *Fortitude* would be gone now too." Denny paused in heavy silence, but the idle movements of his fingers over his coat betrayed his calm. Marvin twitched, furious. What an act this was! "If you're right, I must contact my director and the Getty's board of trustees as soon as possible, of course."

Marvin could hear the anguished tones of Christina's response, and remembered that *Fortitude* had been on loan from Denny's museum. It didn't even belong to the Met. That would make Christina's horror and guilt all the more keen, he knew.

Denny listened for a minute, then said, "No, no, I saw the care you took, I was there with you. You mustn't be so hard on yourself, Christina. I still — to be completely frank, I still don't understand how it could have happened. James's likeness was remarkable, but . . . you're certain the original is gone?"

Oh, what a liar he was! Marvin could barely contain himself.

"Yes, yes. I'm so sorry, my dear. It's just unthinkable. Have you notified museum personnel? The police?" Denny waited. "All right, that makes sense. I'll come immediately, and we'll do it together. Perhaps you're mistaken after all, Christina. Oh . . . James is there now?" He frowned slightly. "He did? Hmmm . . . yes . . . I see."

Marvin felt a wave of gratitude sweep through him. James was there! If only he could get to James, he would figure out how to explain everything. There had to be a way to save Dürer's lovely masterpieces before they were lost forever.

"I'll meet you in your office in twenty minutes," Denny continued. "We'll speak to your director together." He clicked off his phone and reached for his jacket.

This was his chance, Marvin realized. As Denny gathered his coat from the chair, Marvin ran awkwardly to the edge of the desk, careful not to bump the rolled label that was affixed to his belly, and dove straight through the air toward one sleeve.

His body was much heavier than usual, and he barely reached his target. Desperately pedaling his legs, he clutched the fabric just as Denny yanked the jacket over his shoulders.

Denny turned to the table, smiling down at the drawings. "And now, ladies, I can't very well leave you out in the open for anyone to see."

He strode over to the study's closet and removed the briefcase and a fistful of packaging materials. Very gently, with surgical precision, he set about wrapping the drawings in protective paper and laying them flat inside the briefcase. Small as they were, they fit quite easily. Then he clicked the briefcase shut and returned it to the closet.

Marvin watched in silent dread. He could only pray that this was not the last view he'd have of *Justice, Fortitude, Prudence,* and *Temperance.*

A minute later, he found himself clinging

to the jacket sleeve as Denny hurried out the door to the Met.

WITH THE HELP OF A FRIEND

After a brisk walk that seemed to cover ten or twelve blocks — Marvin noted with relief that they were close enough to the museum not to need taxis or subways — Denny ran up the stairs of the Met and finally strode through the door of Christina's office. There, Marvin took in the dismal scene with one glance. James and Karl both looked stricken. Christina was sitting at the table, her blond head bowed, her hands covering her face. Her glasses were strewn in front of her, and her cheeks were wet with tears.

"My career is over," she said. "Over. Who will ever understand this? How could I have done such a terrible thing?"

"Christina," Denny said soothingly, "let's be sure first. I've talked to you at least six times since the drawing left the museum, and up until now, everything was going as planned. I just can't believe you made a mistake."

Marvin listened in disgust. How convincing Denny sounded in his concern.

"Look at it," Christina said dully.

As soon as Denny walked over to her, Marvin crawled down his sleeve to one of his pants legs, and from there to the floor. The bunched-up label made this journey quite arduous, but as soon as he was safely down, he scrambled beneath the table. Now, the question was how to get James's attention.

He could try crawling up to his wrist, as he'd done before, but everyone was so focused on the drawing, he didn't know if James would even notice him. He crouched near the table leg, mulling over this new challenge. Above him, he could hear the tense conversation.

"They looked the same," James was saying. "Nobody could tell them apart."

Christina sighed. "That's why I wanted you to come. I was hoping you'd say I was wrong. But . . . oh, just look at it. As soon as the FBI said they'd retrieved the tracking device from a cab in a taxi yard, I had a sick feeling in my stomach. I had to check the original, to reassure myself. And then . . . well, I knew. You can tell, too, can't you, Denny?"

Of course he can! Marvin wanted to shout. *He planned the entire thing!* He couldn't bear to see Denny's sympathetic nod. "It's not the Dürer," he said quietly.

Christina turned to James, inconsolable. "You see? We could run all sorts of tests to confirm it, but we don't need to. When you've looked at his work for as long as Denny and I have, you can feel it in your bones." She shook her head. "It's that way with any forgery. Whatever the tests say, it's human judgment we all rely on for the final verdict. Because when you know an artist well, the thing that bothers you about a fake will continue to bother you the longer you look at it. Until it becomes unbearable."

Marvin saw her look at his drawing and close her eyes, and he flinched with the realization that something he'd made could cause anyone such grief. But before he had much time to contemplate this, he glimpsed something shiny by the table leg. It was the metal tack he'd hidden the night he was abandoned in Christina's office.

Aha! A weapon. Or, if not a weapon, an

278

excellent poking tool. Marvin grabbed it with his front two legs. Holding the sharp point aloft, and still carrying the folded label, he crawled with great difficulty over to James's sneaker. He climbed up the side of the sneaker, under the edge of James's jeans, and pressed the tack against the boy's bare ankle.

No response. The distressed conversation above continued.

Marvin tensed his leg muscles and vigorously plunged the point of the tack into pale flesh.

"OW!" James yelped.

"What is it?" Karl asked in concern.

"Ow, I don't know, my ankle hurts." James hopped on one foot, almost knocking Marvin to the floor. He dropped to his knee and lifted his pants leg.

"Did you twist it?" Karl started to crouch down next to him, but James had already spied Marvin.

"No, no, Dad. It's okay," James said quickly. "My foot must have fallen asleep. Pins and needles." He looked at Marvin, took the tack and dropped it on the floor, and then surreptitiously placed the beetle under his jacket cuff.

Marvin released a long breath. So far, so good. Now he just had to show James the

address label. From his new position, he could see Denny examining the drawing on the table in front of Christina. It was framed identically to the original, but even through the glass, Marvin had no trouble recognizing it as his own work.

"I just don't understand it," Christina said. "I was so careful. I checked the drawing a dozen times. I don't know how I could have confused them."

Karl crouched next to Christina, his hand

on her shoulder. "They looked so much alike," he said gently. "The museum wouldn't fire you over one mistake."

She raised her eyes despairingly. "Denny, tell them. That drawing was worth at least half a million dollars. On loan from another institution! And I put it at risk needlessly, for my own stupid purposes."

Karl shook his head. "No, that's not fair. You were trying to recover the one that was stolen — *Justice.* It was a good plan."

"It was, Christina, and we all gave it our blessing," Denny said. "But I'm afraid this won't do much for relations between our two museums. The truth is, we were both responsible for the drawing, and we'll both pay the price for this . . . disaster."

Marvin could hardly stand this show of contrition.

Christina gestured at the table, then pressed her fingers into her temples. "I don't even care about my job. The worst thing is that *Fortitude* is gone, and it's my fault."

Karl rubbed her shoulder. "Maybe the FBI will be able to recover it," he said. "I know the microchip fell off or was taken off or whatever, but at least they know where the drawing was up until that point, right?"

"Yes, but it was in a series of public places

— a hotel, a church, an office building. The tracking device isn't precise enough to pinpoint rooms, and the drawing never stopped moving for more than a few minutes, so the FBI didn't have time to close in on the location. Or at least not until the cab returned to the cab yard and they discovered the matting and the microchip on the floor of the backseat. They're still searching, and retracing the path — but I haven't much hope."

"We need to start notifying people," Denny said quietly.

"Yes." Christina sounded hopeless. "I just wanted to give the FBI a little more time, in case . . . Oh, Denny, I can't bear this."

"I know, my dear. I'm so very, very sorry."

This was too much for Marvin. He couldn't stand the drawn look of fear and sadness on Christina's face. As if reading his mind, James blurted, "I have to go to the bathroom."

Karl barely glanced at him. "Okay, buddy. You know where it is."

As soon as they'd left the office, James lifted his wrist and brought Marvin inches from his face. "Where have you BEEN? I couldn't figure out what happened to you! Were you in the museum? Did you get knocked off my arm somehow?" He shook his head. "We've got to think of a safer way to carry you around. Oh my gosh, I thought I'd lost you again."

Looking James straight in the eyes, Marvin promptly rolled on one side, exposing the rolled label.

James stared at him. "What is that?" he asked.

Marvin used his front legs to wiggle the label out from under its belt. He held it out to James.

"It looks like a little piece of paper," James said. "All rolled up. Like a spitball. Is it a spitball?"

Marvin waited.

"Is there something on it?"

Marvin ran enthusiastically from James's wrist to his hand.

"Okay, okay." James crouched down in the hallway, leaning against the wall. He took the label with two fingers and turned his hand over slowly so that Marvin wouldn't fall off.

"What am I supposed to do with it?" he asked, watching Marvin. "Open it up?" He began to unroll the miniature paper bundle. When he was finished, he spread the crinkled white rectangle on his thigh and looked at it.

"Gordon Perry, 236 East 74th Street,

Apartment 5D, New York, New York," he read.

Marvin frowned. Uh-oh. So the label didn't have Denny's name on it, after all. But surely that was still the correct apartment. Seventy-fourth Street made sense, just blocks from the Met.

"Who is this?" James asked, studying Marvin intently.

Marvin ran around excitedly.

"What's the matter? Why are you so excited?" James watched Marvin with his serious gray eyes. "Do what you did before, when I gave you a ride to the kitchen. Go to the end of my finger if I'm right. Does this guy have something to do with the drawing? The real drawing?"

Marvin raced to the tip of James's finger.

"Yes? Did he steal the drawing?"

Well, that wasn't quite right, but James was so smart, he would figure it out.

"Really?" James bit his lip. "What should we do? Call the police?"

Marvin retreated to the middle of James's knuckle. No, no, that wouldn't work. The police would have no idea what to do with this information, and no reason to believe it mattered.

James looked at the label, his brow furrowing. "I don't know, little guy."

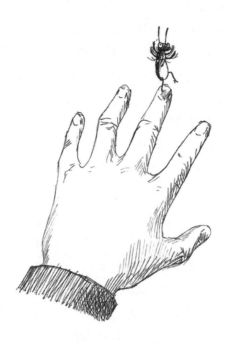

Marvin ran to the tip of James's finger and stretched his legs out over the air.

"You want me to take you somewhere? Where?"

Marvin waved his legs frantically.

"Okay, I get it. Where? To this address?"

Good for James! Marvin knew he would understand. He stayed at the tip of James's finger, waving two legs in the air.

"But what if this guy is the thief?"

Marvin continued to thrust himself forward into space, willing James to get up on his feet and in motion.

James cast a sideways glance at Christina's door. "Should I tell them?"

Alarmed, Marvin crawled back to James's knuckle. He could only imagine what would happen if Denny found out they were on their way to the place where Dürer's masterpieces lay hidden.

"No?" James sighed. "I guess you're right. They won't understand, and then they won't let me go."

He stood up, thinking. "Okay, look, it's not far from here. My dad will totally freak out, so we can't be gone long. I don't even know what you want me to do, but maybe you can show me when we get there." Marvin returned delightedly to his fingertip.

James looked down at him anxiously. "Is this going to be dangerous?"

That sounded so similar to something Marvin himself would say to Elaine that he almost smiled, despite his jangled nerves. As long as Denny was there at the museum, they were safe. He hoped. He looked up at James, not knowing how to respond. Getting to the apartment was only half the battle, Marvin knew. Then he had to figure out a way to get James to the drawings.

Clutching the label in his fist, James scrambled to his feet, tucked Marvin under the cuff of his jacket, and ran down the hall toward the exit.

BREAKING AND ENTERING

James walked much more quickly than Marvin had expected, covering the dozen blocks to the apartment on East Seventy-fourth Street in long strides. When they got to the large front stoop, he hesitated, shivering, as he scanned the metal panel of apartment numbers and buzzers. It had started to snow lightly, wet flakes dusting the sidewalk.

"What should I do? Push the button?" he asked Marvin. Marvin crawled to the tip of his finger, but with no particular enthusiasm. He knew the apartment was empty.

"Let's see, 5D," James said. He read the label again. "Perry. Here it is." He pressed. There was no response.

James bounced on his sneakers. He looked up at the tall front of the building, blinking away snowflakes. Then he shrugged. "I guess we have to find a way inside, huh? Somebody must be home in one of these places."

He dragged his fingers over the double row of buttons, hitting every one. The intercom crackled, with multiple voices sputtering, "Yes?" and "Who is it?" until someone indifferently pressed the release button and the front door buzzed. Quickly, James turned the handle and pushed his way into the small tiled lobby.

They rode the elevator to the fifth floor, with Marvin trying to think how to get into the apartment. He could certainly crawl under the door, but that wouldn't help James. Once inside, he supposed he might be able to set off the fire alarm (Uncle Albert, the electrical whiz, had taught Marvin a few tricks), and if he succeeded, the building super was sure to come and open the door for a look around. But how would

James explain what he was doing there?

James found the door marked with a brass plate showing "5D." He looked nervously down the hallway. "Okay, I guess I'll knock," he told Marvin. "There'd better not be some *criminal* in here."

He took a deep breath and tapped on the door. There was no answer. He looked down at Marvin. "Now what do we do?"

Marvin ran to James's fingertip and waved his front legs at the door.

"I know, I know. You want to go inside. But how?" James tried the door handle with both hands. "See, it's locked."

Marvin, seeing his chance, crawled quickly onto the doorknob. The only thing he could think to do was to try to spring the lock himself. He took a good, long look into the blackness of the keyhole, then plunged inside.

"Wait! What are you doing?" James protested.

The keyhole was dark and crowded with chunks of cold metal. Marvin could see the workings of the lock with perfect clarity, but he had no idea how to move the mechanism and unlock the door. Great-aunt Mildred, the family locksmith, had given several lectures to the relatives on exactly this topic, but Marvin hadn't realized he'd need the information so soon himself. The secret was some kind of leverage, as he recalled.

"Hey!" James whispered through the keyhole, sending a warm blast of air rushing into the tiny space. "Where are you, little guy?"

Marvin saw one of James's worried eyes appear in the opening. "Are you trying to open it? Really? That would be so cool!"

Marvin pushed as hard as he could against the metal bolt, but it wouldn't budge.

A minute later, James's breath swooshed into the keyhole again. "Guess what? I have a paper clip in my pocket! Maybe that will help. Hold on."

Marvin heard him rustling, and a moment later, the curved wire end of a paper clip came thrusting into the keyhole. Marvin leapt out of the way right before it skewered him. *Take it easy,* he thought.

"Does that help?" James whispered.

Marvin considered the paper clip and the metal bar of the lock. He tried desperately to recall Great-aunt Mildred's instructions. He positioned the paper clip carefully against the mechanism of the lock, then turned himself around and pressed the back of his shell against the paper clip. Wedging his feet against the bar of the lock, he pushed as hard as he could.

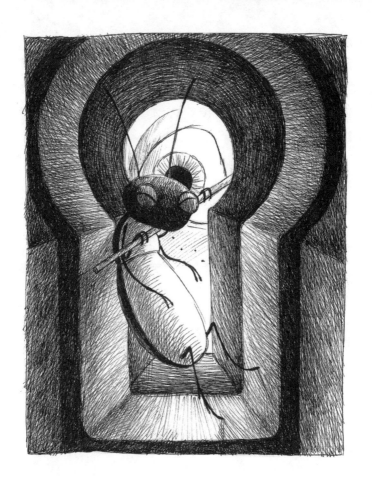

Nothing.

He pushed again.

Nothing.

"How's it going?" James whispered.
"Maybe you aren't strong enough on your
own. I'll try turning the paper clip, okay?"

Marvin repositioned the paper clip and
pushed with all his might just as James
began to twist it. Leverage! He heard a dull
thunk as the metal bar slid back.

"It's unlocked!" James whispered in delight, opening the door. Marvin scrambled out of the keyhole and onto James's hand. A moment later, they were inside the apartment.

A REVELATION

James closed the door softly behind them. He flipped the light switch, surveying the small, tidy living room of the apartment.

"What is this place?" he asked Marvin. "Who's Gordon Perry?"

Who, indeed. A friend of Denny's? An accomplice in the theft? Marvin had no idea. He moved to the tip of James's finger and once again dangled his legs in the air.

"Where do you want to go now?" James asked. He began to walk slowly around the living room.

Using the technique they'd perfected earlier, Marvin guided James, with a few false stops and starts, to the closed door of the study.

"Okay," James said. "In here." He opened the door and stepped inside. "Huh."

He looked around, scanning the bookshelves and table. Then he walked to the desk, glancing at the stack of mail. "This is his place, all right. But there's nothing here, little guy. What do we do now?" He hesitated in front of the window, staring gloomily out at the falling snow. "I have to go back. My dad will be really worried, and if he calls my mom . . . well, you know how she is."

No! Not yet, James, Marvin begged. He ran back and forth along James's finger.

"Okay, relax. What are you trying to tell me?"

James turned toward the closet, where Marvin was pointing himself. "Something in there?"

Marvin scurried to the end of James's finger and drummed all his legs in place, doing a frantic dance.

His brow furrowing, James crossed the room and opened the closet door, revealing a jumble of coats and a few packing boxes. The briefcase was on the floor in the back.

Marvin flung his front legs over the precipice of James's fingertip, waving them in midair.

"What?" James asked, squatting on his

294

heels. "It's just a bunch of boxes. What are you so excited about?"

Marvin whirled in circles, desperate for James to discover Denny's secret.

"Is it something about the drawing?"

Overcome with frustration, Marvin hurled himself from James's finger to the floor and ran across the wooden boards to the brief-case.

"Oh," James said. "That thing? Okay, let's see."

He picked up Marvin very gently and tugged the briefcase out of the closet. Sitting cross-legged on the floor, he set it on its side and flipped the latches.

"It's just a bunch of papers," he said.

Marvin dove off his finger once again, landing smack in the middle of the packaging that surrounded the drawings.

"Listen, little guy. We have to go back to the museum. I don't know what you think is here, but —"

Marvin pounded on the top layer of paper with his legs, thoroughly beside himself.

James took a deep breath. "I don't think I should mess around with this stuff. That Perry guy will notice and get mad."

Marvin rolled onto his back and waved all six legs in the air, as dramatic an SOS sign as he could think of.

"Geez," James said. "You're going crazy." He touched the edge of the top paper with his fingers. With all his might, Marvin flipped himself onto his stomach and ran to the edge of the sheet.

James shifted it aside and hesitantly unwrapped what was underneath. He gasped.

There, unveiled in all its glory, was *Fortitude.*

James stared. "It's the real one," he said haltingly, as if he couldn't trust his own eyes. "It is, isn't it?" He looked down at Marvin in amazement. "You found it! The one that was stolen! How did you do that?"

James sprang to his feet, trembling. He began to pace around the table, gripping his head with both hands and talking so fast that Marvin could barely keep up. "The Perry guy must have taken it! We have to tell my dad. We have to tell Christina and Denny. What if he comes back? What if he finds us here?"

Suddenly, James reached down and plucked Marvin from the paper, positioning him snugly under his cuff. He looked around the room. Spying the phone on the desk, he rushed to it.

"We'll call my dad," he said. "He'll know what to do." He punched the numbers and

held the phone tightly against his cheek, waiting.

After a minute, he groaned. "It's not going through. He must be someplace where his cell phone doesn't work."

Marvin tried to think what to do. But James didn't hesitate. He punched in more numbers. "Hello? Um, New York City. Can I have the phone number for the Met? Yeah,

the museum. No, wait! Not the recording, I need a real person. Yeah, that's good. Thanks." He wrote a number on the pad of paper on the desk, then dialed it. "Hi, uh, can you connect me to Christina Balcony's office?"

James's voice exploded with excitement.

"Denny! Denny, it's me, James! I found the drawing! I found *Fortitude*!"

TRAPPED

Marvin froze. Denny! *Don't tell Denny,* he wanted to scream.

But of course James had no way of knowing that Denny was the thief. He was already babbling ecstatically into the phone. "No, really! I'm in somebody's apartment, this guy Gordon Perry. The address is" — here James read from the crinkled label — "236 East 74th Street, Apartment 5D."

No! Don't tell him! Marvin raced onto James's hand.

"It's the real one. I know it is. I . . . I can't explain on the phone. Can you get my dad?" There was a long pause.

"Oh," James said, "he is? Okay, but you'll

tell him, and Christina too? And can you please hurry? I don't know when this guy might come back."

He hung up and looked down triumphantly at Marvin. "We did it!" he crowed, dancing around the table. "Dad and Christina weren't there — they'd gone to look for me — but Denny's going to find them and tell them, and then they'll all come over here. Everything's going to be fine!"

Oh, no! Marvin slumped in despair. This was impossible. How could he make James understand that they were in terrible danger?

Nobody knew they were here but Denny. And Denny, the real thief, was on his way to the apartment. He certainly wouldn't tell Karl or Christina anything. Marvin trembled. What would he do with the drawings when he got here? More important, what would he do with James?

James lifted his hand and peered at Marvin, tilting his head to one side. "What's the matter, little guy? You don't seem very happy."

Marvin took a deep breath, trying to shake off his hopelessness. He had to convince James to leave the apartment. And to take the drawings with him! But how?

He crawled to the end of James's finger

and motioned with his front legs.

"Where do you want to go now?" James asked, looking at him quizzically. "I think we should just wait till they all get here."

Marvin continued to gesture toward the briefcase.

James walked doubtfully over to the closet and crouched on the floor, holding out his hand so Marvin could disembark. Marvin crawled straight to the part of the briefcase with the handle and latches, and waited there expectantly.

"You want me to shut it again?" James asked.

Marvin climbed onto one of the latches.

"Why? Denny and Dad and Christina are on their way here. Can't we let them do it?"

Marvin tapped his front legs imperatively.

James paused. "I'm scared I'll wreck the drawing." When Marvin didn't budge, he sighed. "You can be really bossy, do you know that?" He fiddled with the packaging sheets. "But I guess you've been right about most things so far. And you did find the drawing."

He sighed again. "Okay, watch out." Gently, he wrapped the paper sheets over *Fortitude* and, while Marvin clung to the latch, closed the briefcase.

Marvin was about to jump off when he

301

caught sight of something under the brief-case's handle. Imprinted in the worn leather, faintly traced in gold. What was it?

Letters, he realized. Three of them. Faded almost beyond recognition.

Something stirred in a remote part of Marvin's brain; something from the human world. Three letters on Mrs. Pompaday's bathroom towels. Three letters on Mr. Pompaday's silver cuff links. Three letters on the pen case that Karl gave James for his birthday. ("Look, your initials, so everyone will know it's yours.")

Initials. Denny's initials.

Marvin went crazy. He leapt in the air, rolled over, waved all his legs, and spun in a mad circle. *Here! Look, James! Now you'll know!*

The letters were so faded and small that only a beetle would ever notice them. A beetle and a boy who always paid attention.

"You're doing it again," James said in amazement. "Calm down! What's wrong with you? Maybe you're having a seizure, like Billy Dunwood did after he got hit by that baseball last summer."

Marvin crouched directly above the initials and pounded his front legs on the leather.

"Oh," James said. "Yeah, I see it. Some-body's initials." He bent over the briefcase

and squinted. "So what? I can't even read them. 'D,' something, 'D.E.M.' Is that what you wanted me to see? Why? Why do you care about that?"

Marvin stayed right where he was, determined not to move until James made the connection. He continued to tap his front legs.

"D.E.M. Okay. Who is that?" James asked him. "I guess it's not Gordon Perry. But he could have borrowed somebody else's briefcase. Or maybe this is the guy who helped him steal the drawing."

Marvin spun in a circle and waved his legs madly.

"That's it? This is the guy who helped him steal *Fortitude*? Okay, but I don't know anybody with the initials —" James stopped. He squinted at the top of the briefcase, angling it toward him. "What's this?" he asked, tracing his finger over a square insignia printed on the leather. Marvin saw it, too, on the top of the case, a small box with symbols inside it.

"It's letters too," James said. "G-E-T-T-Y," he read. "Getty. Wait, isn't that Denny's museum? Out in California?" His gray eyes widened.

Turning to Marvin, he whispered, "What's Denny's last name again? Mac- something. MacGuffin." He shook his head. "But why would he . . . He couldn't have. He was the one who —"

Please, Marvin begged silently. If there was such a thing as mind reading, he needed James to do it right now.

James stopped again, then sucked in his breath. "Oh, my gosh! If it *is* Denny, he's coming. . . . We have to get out of here!"

Yes! Finally, he understood. Marvin leapt onto James's outstretched hand and scooted under his jacket cuff. In a panic, James grabbed the handle of the briefcase and ran to the door of the apartment.

They rushed into the hallway just as the

elevator dinged.

"What if it's Denny?" James whispered, frantic. He whirled around. "We have to take the stairs. Where are they?"

As the elevator doors began to open, he ran down the hall toward a broad metal door with a lit-up red sign over it.

Hurry, Marvin thought, *hurry!*

James pushed through the door into a narrow, bleak stairwell. He thudded down the first flight of stairs, the briefcase banging against his legs.

"I hope he didn't see us. I hope he didn't see us," he kept whispering to Marvin, like a magical incantation, as he rounded the corner and took the second flight of stairs two steps at a time. Marvin clung to the jacket cloth, bouncing helplessly against James's wrist, craning to see if they were being followed.

Finally, they came to the first floor and burst into the lobby.

James raced across the entryway, heaved open the massive front door, and ran down the steps to the sidewalk. Outside, he paused only a moment, then took off down the street through the fast-falling snow.

REUNION

Marvin shrank back from the chill and scrambled farther underneath the jacket cuff, poking out just enough of his head to see. He was so exhausted from his prolonged bout of sign language that he could hardly think what to do next.

Fortunately, James seemed filled with purpose. He yanked his hood over his head and told Marvin, "We have to call my dad. Maybe his cell phone is working now. It'd better be."

He trotted down the slippery sidewalk to a restaurant on the street corner. Inside, a hostess stood at the front desk with a sheaf of menus in her hand.

"Um, excuse me," James said shyly. "Could I . . . do you think I could . . ."

The woman bent down, smiling. "What is it, honey? Where's your mother? Are you meeting someone here?"

James shook his head, blushing. "Could I use your phone? Please?"

"Oh! Are you lost? Of course you can. Come back here." She beckoned him behind the desk and lifted the receiver, pressing a button. "There, that's the outside line. Do you know your phone number?"

James nodded, biting his lip. Quickly, he dialed.

Marvin heard his joyful exhalation, and felt a rush of relief.

"Dad! Dad, it's you." There was a long pause on James's end while Karl's anxious exclamations cascaded through the phone line. "No, I'm okay, Dad. Everything's okay. Sorry. Sorry, I — No, I'm not in the museum — Dad, listen —" Marvin heard James groan in frustration. "Dad, wait in Christina's office. I'm coming right now, okay? Just wait there." James plunked the phone back into its cradle and turned to the door.

"Where are you going, honey?" the hostess asked. "Don't you want to wait here?"

"No, it's okay," James mumbled. "Thanks

for letting me use the phone." He awkwardly swung the briefcase aside as he reached for the door handle.

"But —" she started to protest. Before she could stop him, James slipped out into the street.

He ran the whole way to the museum, sneakers thudding against the wet pavement, Marvin clinging to his wrist. He stopped only for the walk signals at the end of each block. It was evening now, and the cottony gray sky had darkened, yielding to the deep blue of another winter night. The snow fell steadily, at first melting when it struck the ground, then gradually dusting and coating everything it touched. From his snug hiding place, Marvin watched this transformation with wide eyes. By the time they reached the museum, a veil of white shrouded the city, softening its edges, quieting its sounds, as welcome as a benediction.

As soon as James walked through the front entrance of the museum, he was stopped by one of the security guards.

"Wait right there, son," the man said, clapping a beefy hand on his shoulder. "What's your name?"

"James Terik," James answered nervously.

"I thought it was you!" the guard boomed. "Your father is going to be mighty glad to

see you. Security's been combing the place. Good thing they told us what color jacket you were wearing." He unhooked a radio transmitter from his belt and spoke into it. "Ed? I've got the Terik kid. Yeah, right here at the main entrance. They are? Okay, I'll take him up."

He turned to James. "Your dad is upstairs in Ms. Balcony's office. Let's go. What have you got there?" He pointed to the briefcase.

"Oh . . . just something for my dad,"

James said quickly.

When James walked through the door of Christina's office, he was immediately engulfed in Karl's tight embrace, and Christina rushed over to them.

"James! James, where were you? You scared me, buddy! I thought something had happened to you." Karl crouched down, gripping James's shoulders. "You can't go off like that. We've been looking everywhere for you."

Marvin, peeking out from under the jacket cuff, could see that Christina's pretty face was pinched with worry. "Oh, James, I'm so glad you're all right! We've lost too much today already."

"I know, I'm sorry," James said, burrowing into his father's chest. "But it was something important. I —" He took a deep breath and stepped back, looking at both of them. "I found *Fortitude*."

"WHAT?" Christina and Karl spoke in unison, staring at him.

"Here," James said simply, holding up the briefcase. It dangled in the air, scuffed and innocuous. Nobody made a move to take it.

"Look inside," James said.

Karl frowned, lifting the briefcase and setting it on the table. He unlatched and

opened it, looking at the layers of protective
paper.

"What's this?" he asked James. "Whose is
it?"

Christina's brow furrowed. "It's
Denny's . . . isn't it? Where did you get this,
James?"

"Look," James said again.

It was Christina who moved forward now,
lifting the protective wrapping. Suddenly,
she stopped, her hand gripping the edge of
the table.

Marvin scrambled up James's sleeve to his
collar for a better view.

"Karl," Christina said.

"What is it?"

"You do it."

Karl removed the last sheet.

"Oh, my God," he said.

Keep going, Marvin wanted to say. You're about to see the four *Virtues* together for the first time in decades. Centuries maybe.

But Karl needed no encouragement. Gently, with held breath, he removed the tiny drawing. He turned to Christina. "It's the real one, isn't it?"

She couldn't take her eyes off it. When she nodded, he removed the remaining packaging.

"Oh, my God," he said again. "Christina . . . Christina, it's all of them."

Marvin saw Christina's knees buckle, and Karl caught her elbow to keep her from falling.

"How can that be?" she asked, her voice barely audible.

"I don't know," Karl said, turning to James, who pressed against him, his face a blur of confusion. "But it is. Look." He set the four drawings in a row on the table. *"Fortitude. Temperance. Prudence. Justice."*

"Oh!" Christina gasped.

Karl kept his arm around her, holding her up. He looked at James for an answer.

James, red-faced and wide-eyed, stared at the drawings. Marvin huddled under the jacket collar, afraid to move.

Christina bent over the table, her eyes following each graceful line.

"I can't believe —" The words caught in her throat. "They're all here!"

THE THIEF OF *VIRTUE*

They gazed at Dürer's four *Virtues*. Marvin felt again the thrill that had coursed through him when he first saw them in Denny's study.

Karl squinted at the miniature images. "Are you sure they're the real ones?" he asked Christina. "The ones that were stolen?"

Christina nodded, unable to speak. Her eyes moved from one figure to the next, stopping at the picture of *Justice.*

"Look at it," she said. "I thought I'd never see it again."

She walked along the edge of the table, holding her breath. "And *Prudence*! And

Temperance! They've been missing for more than two years."

Together at last, the drawings had a pulsing energy that filled the room like music rising. Of course they were real, Marvin thought. There was no mistaking them.

Christina turned to James. "How on earth . . . I don't understand. How did you find them?"

James bit his lip.

"Where did you get this briefcase, James?" Karl asked quietly.

James shifted from one foot to the other, his gray eyes anxious. "It was in an apartment," he said finally. He took the crinkled label out of his jeans pocket and set it on the table.

Christina picked it up, her brow furrowing. "This is Gordon Perry's place."

James hesitated. "I think he's the one who took the drawings."

"Now hold on — who's Gordon Perry?" Karl asked.

"One of our curators," Christina said. "But what do you mean, James? Gordon's in Florence, helping with restoration work at the Uffizi. He's been there for a month. Denny's staying at his place."

James chewed his bottom lip, watching her.

"Where *is* Denny?" Karl asked impatiently. "We have to tell him what's happened."

"Yes, of course, I'll call him now." Christina lifted the phone on her desk.

"He already knows," James said.

Both Christina and Karl turned to James, staring at him so intently now that Marvin felt obliged to duck back under James's collar lest he be seen.

"What are you talking about?" Karl asked.

James swallowed and stared at the floor, but Christina crouched in front of him, her voice coaxing. "James, what is it?"

"I told Denny already. I called here and told him about *Fortitude,* and he said he'd go get you . . ." James stopped. "But he didn't."

Christina put her hands on his shoulders and looked straight into his eyes. Marvin cringed at the bewildered sincerity in her

face. How could he ever have doubted her? He felt a wave of guilt. She deserved an honest answer. But what would James say? It was all too hard to explain.

"James, you have to tell us what's going on," Christina continued. "How did you find these drawings? Why do you have this briefcase?"

"Listen," James began, and Marvin knew

he was assembling the details in his mind, his imagination rushing to fill each pause. "When we came this morning and Christina showed us my drawing, I found that address. Right here, rolled up . . . on the floor." James pointed vaguely under the table. "I had this weird feeling. I can't explain it. I figured the address had something to do with the drawing. I thought maybe it had fallen off the paper, you know, the package that was supposed to have the real *Fortitude* inside." James glanced at them desperately.

Even Marvin felt confused at this point, and he could tell from their faces that Karl and Christina were thoroughly baffled. The story was sounding more implausible the longer James talked.

"Anyway," James continued lamely, looking at the floor, "it was like a mailing label. It seemed important. But I figured you wouldn't believe me if I told you, Dad, so that's why I left without saying anything." He took a deep breath and plunged into the rest of the tale.

"And then I found *Fortitude* in that apartment. I tried to call you, Dad, but your cell phone wasn't working. So I had to call here, and Denny answered the phone. It was, I don't know, about an hour ago. I said where

I was, and I told Denny about the drawing. And he . . . he said he'd tell you and you'd all come right away."

James stopped, raising his eyes slowly to their faces. "But he didn't tell you, did he? I think he didn't tell you because he stole the drawings. They were in that Gordon Perry guy's apartment. In Denny's briefcase."

"James," Karl said. His voice was sterner than Marvin had ever heard it. "That's a terrible accusation to make."

"I know, Dad, but —"

Karl shook his head. "Denny's been my friend for years. I'm sure there's an explanation."

James stared miserably at the briefcase. "Look, it has the sign for the Getty museum on it . . . and Denny's initials," he mumbled, gesturing.

Christina was still kneeling next to him, but her gaze shifted back to the briefcase, then to the drawings. She was silent for a long time.

"Denny helped with the entire theft," she said finally. "He knew every detail of the arrangements we'd made . . . the timing, where the microchip would be hidden, the name of the undercover FBI agent."

Karl stared at her. "So? You knew those things too."

Christina shook her head slightly, as if she was trying to puzzle out something.

"It's Denny we're talking about!" Karl protested.

"Yes," Christina said. She stood. "He was with me the night I switched the drawings. We were the only two in the museum at that hour, besides the security staff."

"Right," Karl said. "But that doesn't make him a thief."

"When we made the exchange, I brought the real Dürer here to my office. Denny was with me. I wrapped it up, and . . . oh, I don't know, how can it be? It's *Denny,* he couldn't have done this."

"No! He's not a thief."

"But listen to me," Christina said pensively. "He was with me, but we were also, I don't know, apart at different times. He could have changed the wrapping. He was the one who hung James's drawing down in the gallery while I took the real Dürer, or what I thought was the real Dürer, up to the fifth floor, to the vault in the director's office."

"Christina —" Karl interrupted.

"I know, I know. It's so hard to believe." She lapsed into silence again, staring at the drawings. "Karl . . . today, when I told him *Fortitude* was gone . . . there was something

321

wrong with the way he reacted. He was upset, certainly, but he seemed almost more concerned about me. And I kept thinking, 'This is so strange, one of the Getty's prized artworks may be lost forever, and he's telling me how sorry he is.' "

"Well, of course, he *was* sorry," Karl exclaimed. "He loves Dürer's work, and he knows you do too."

"Yes," Christina said. She sighed. "This is his briefcase, I'm sure of it. Look — 'D.E.M.,' and the Getty logo." She lifted her phone. "I think we need to talk to Denny himself."

James watched her anxiously, and Marvin poked his head farther out, wanting to hear what Denny would possibly say.

Christina pursed her lips. "He's not picking up his cell." After a minute, she said, "Denny, hi, it's Christina. Please call me as soon as you get this message. It's important." She turned to Karl. "Let's try the apartment," she said, dialing again.

Karl and James stood tensely, waiting. After a minute, she shook her head. "He's not answering there either."

Christina set down the phone, her eyes settling on *Fortitude.* "I was so busy all day yesterday, talking to the FBI, going over everything. I wasn't even in the museum for most of it. Of course, I didn't think I needed to double-check the drawing. We'd been so careful in my office. And I trusted him! Completely. I even asked him a couple of times to make sure everything looked all right, and he said it did."

Karl shook his head. "I don't believe it. Denny . . . he's a good man. He's as devoted to Dürer as you are."

Christina nodded. "More so."

"Then why? Why gamble his entire career, not to mention a prison sentence?"

"Will he go to jail?" James interrupted, his eyes wide.

Maybe he deserves to go to jail, Marvin thought.

But Karl didn't answer, still focused on Christina. "As a practical matter, where would he even get the money to buy one of these?"

Christina hesitated. "Well, Denny comes from money. And who knows? Maybe he's the front man for someone else."

Marvin thought back to the apartment, to Denny's conversation with the woman with the funny-sounding name. Something about being picked up at an airport.

"On the black market," Christina continued, "the drawings would cost considerably less than their real value. Dürer is not nearly

323

as well known as the bigger names of the Renaissance, and these can't be resold anywhere legitimate."

Karl paced the room, while James watched them both with huge eyes. "But it just doesn't make sense. *Fortitude* was at the Getty already. Why not steal it from there? Why wait till it was all the way across the country?"

"That's the part that *does* make sense," Christina said slowly. "He was much less likely to get caught here. The drawing was on loan to the Met, we were the ones responsible. Oh, my God!" She covered her mouth. "*Justice*! Denny was here in New York when it was stolen. He was at a conference. He came to the Met all the time that week. He had full access to the departments. I made sure of that." She shook her head. "I couldn't have made this easier for him if I'd tried."

"You think he stole *all* of the drawings?" Karl asked, stunned.

"I don't know," Christina said soberly. "Maybe he hired people to take the first two." She rested her hand weakly next to *Fortitude*. "With this one, I might as well have presented it to him gift-wrapped."

James looked from one to the other, and Marvin could see that his pale face was pinched and tired. It had been a long day. "But you said he couldn't sell them, right?" he asked. "And he couldn't show them to anybody or tell anybody he had them, because the police would be looking for them. So why did he do this?"

Christina's eyes traced the four tiny images. "Maybe he just wanted them together . . . for himself."

Marvin remembered Denny in the dark study, looking at the drawings with tears in his eyes.

"So what now?" Karl asked Christina. "Are you going to call the FBI?"

"If this is true . . ." Christina winced. "Can you imagine tomorrow's headlines?" It'll be awful for him. And for the two museums. For everyone."

"But will he go to jail?" James asked again.

Karl and Christina were silent. After a minute, Karl said, "Look at the expression on Justice's face," he said. "This is why she looks so sad."

James glanced up at his father, and Karl explained, "Because the right thing to do can be so awful sometimes."

There seemed nothing more to say. Marvin crouched beneath James's collar, his heart heavy.

Karl ran his fingers through his hair. "We

should call the FBI. Tell them about the drawings." He looked at James. "I still don't understand how you found these, James. How'd you even get into the apartment by yourself? How did you know they'd be there?"

James squirmed awkwardly, avoiding his father's eyes. "It's like I said, I found that address and I just knew," he answered softly. "And then when I got there, I used a paper clip to —"

"What?" Karl's mouth dropped open. "You picked the lock?"

"Sort of," James said. Quickly, he turned to Christina, and Marvin knew he was trying to change the subject. "Why can't you just give the drawings back? That's the important thing, anyway. Why do you have to tell the police about Denny?"

Christina touched his hair gently. "It's a crime, James. Think of Dürer's virtues . . . Prudence, Temperance, Fortitude, Justice. Above all, Justice. Don't you think we have a duty to honor those ideals?"

James looked worriedly at Karl. "But those aren't the only good things. What about sticking up for somebody? Isn't that important too? Denny's your friend."

But he did a bad thing, Marvin wanted to protest. He couldn't forget the surge of

326

anger he'd felt listening to Denny's side of the phone conversation when Christina told him the real drawing had been stolen. Denny had lied to her. He'd manipulated all of them.

But then Marvin remembered that James didn't know that. James thought of him only as the kindly, rumpled man who loved Dürer's drawings.

Christina turned to Karl. "The Greeks said the four virtues contained all the rest, remember?"

Karl shook his head. "But they don't. Denny's a good friend. I can't believe he did this, but if it happened . . . what about compassion? What about forgiveness?"

Marvin inched forward again to look at the four miniatures. In their crisp, certain strokes, none of these drawings seemed to capture forgiveness. The images had to do with strength and self-control: the girl fighting the lion, the girl measuring wine, the girl refusing the winged suitor, the girl wielding the sword. Forgiveness was softer and more generous; it was something you offered to another person, rather than something you demanded of yourself.

Christina looked at him for a moment, then said again gently: "It's a crime. And it's not up to us." She picked up the phone.

327

"Who knows? Maybe I'm wrong. Maybe there's an explanation we haven't thought of. But we have to tell the FBI and let them take it from here."

As she dialed, she whispered, "Isn't it amazing to see the *Virtues* together like this, just as Dürer intended?"

Marvin studied each drawing, resplendent in its detail. So much human fuss over something so small. It was somehow heartening to him.

Karl pulled James close to him, squeezing his shoulder. "The FBI will want to talk to you, buddy. But for now, let's go home. Picking locks, finding stolen masterpieces . . . I'd say your work here is done."

Home, Marvin thought. He was immediately overcome with longing for Mama and Papa, for his cotton-ball bed and his smothering, overinvolved relatives — even for Elaine. He couldn't wait to be back where he belonged.

Safe Returns

Marvin's homecoming was a dramatic affair, full of exclamations and recriminations, joyous embraces and stern I-told-you-so's. When James finally lowered him to the bottom of the dark cupboard and he crawled through the plaster wall into his own living room, he was instantly subsumed in a throng of anxious kinfolk, who extended dozens of legs to pat his shell and chuck him under the chin.

"Marvin!" Mama and Papa cried simultaneously, rushing over to him. They couldn't stop hugging him, clearly overcome with guilt at having actually given permission for this last, most dangerous outing.

"My boy, we thought you were done for!" Uncle Albert boomed. "This business of leaving home to help the humans has gone entirely too far."

"Indeed it has," chimed in Marvin's grandmother. "Have you learned nothing from the experiences of your elders, dear boy? You must stop dabbling in human affairs! No good will come of it."

Elaine's eyes were huge. "Oh, Marvin, you don't know how scared we've all been!" she cried. "Why, I just knew the most terrible thing had happened to you. When I heard you'd gone back to the museum again, I said, 'He'll end up drowned in that bottle of ink —' "

"Now, Elaine," Aunt Edith interrupted.

Marvin thought of Elaine in the turtle tank and muttered under his breath, "You know what a good swimmer I am."

But mostly he accepted their concerned scolding without complaint. He was beginning to understand that some of the most irritating things his family did stemmed from the depth of their love. And suddenly it felt wonderful to be worried about and fussed over, to be reclaimed by their messy closeness. Marvin remembered his lonely journey with *Fortitude,* when he thought that he might never see Mama and Papa and the

relatives again. He realized that this was exactly what he had pined for — the thick web of affection that bound them all together. In some fundamental way, whatever terrible or wonderful thing happened to him always seemed to have happened to them, as well.

And so it was that Marvin was obliged to spend the evening telling all about his adventures, every exciting and horrifying detail: about the burglary, the dark trip through the city with *Fortitude,* the discovery of the three other *Virtue* drawings, the shocking revelation that Denny himself had masterminded the heists.

In between the myriad questions and discussions this prompted, Mama and Aunt Edith kept replenishing the table with platters of food — potato peelings, flakes of tuna fish, an orange rind, and crumbs of toast spread with a truly delicious rhubarb jelly — so that by midnight, everyone was well-stuffed and ready for a nap.

"You need to rest, Marvin," Mama said decisively. "All this excitement is too much for you."

"I am pretty tired," Marvin admitted.

Elaine followed him into his room. "You're so lucky," she told him, careful to lower her voice so that the grown-ups wouldn't hear.

Marvin nodded. "I know. I thought I might never be back here again."

"I don't mean that," she said dismissively. "I mean lucky you got out of the apartment again. You've gotten to see the world!"

Marvin thought about that. He *had* seen the world. It had been scary at times, but also exhilarating. Who could have imagined it would be such a complicated, interesting place? Elaine was right — he was lucky. When you saw different parts of the world, you saw different parts of yourself. And when you stayed home, where it was safe, those parts of yourself also stayed hidden.

It wasn't until late the next day that Marvin had a chance to visit James again. He made his way to James's bedroom and found him hunched over his desk, drawing with his ink set. The pictures looked nothing like Marvin's. The strokes were fat and unsteady. The things he drew had an abstract, disjointed look: an angular, foreshortened chair; the thick, pronged branches of the tree outside the window. James was concentrating so hard, he didn't see Marvin crawl to the edge of the paper and stand there, watching. When the boy finally noticed him, he gasped in delight and sheepishly set down his pen.

"Hey!" he said. "Little guy! I never know when you're going to show up. We have to figure out a way to reach each other, you know? Like if I have a special message for you, maybe I can leave something in the cupboard so you know to come here. Or if you really need me, you can do the same thing." He thought for a minute. "Something small . . . I know!"

He tore off a corner of the paper he was drawing on and made an ink X on it. "We'll put this in the kitchen cupboard behind the wastebasket, right by your house. We'll leave it facedown unless one of us needs the other, then we'll turn it over. And if it's turned over, we'll meet here at my desk in the afternoon. Okay? Let's say four o'clock, because I'm always home from school by then."

James nodded emphatically, pleased with himself. Marvin smiled up at him. They might not be able to talk to each other, but there were so many other ways to say what they meant.

James pointed at his picture. "Look what I'm making. I'll never be as good as you are . . . but I like it. It's fun." He lowered his finger and Marvin climbed onto it.

"And guess what. I have so much to tell you. I had to go to the police station! There was a jail and everything! And I talked to the FBI." His face clouded momentarily. "I don't think they believed me, exactly, when I said how I found the drawings. But Christina kind of took over and told them about Denny, and then they let me come home."

James leaned closer to Marvin, lowering

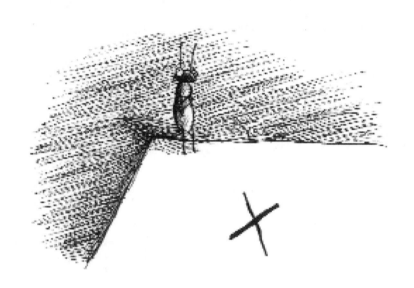

his voice. "The FBI can't find Denny anywhere. When they got to the apartment,
he'd cleaned out all his stuff. He may have
left the country! They think he went to
Germany. Christina keeps calling his cell
phone, and he doesn't answer." James
sighed. "I know what he did was wrong and
everything, but I still kind of hope he
doesn't get caught."

Then he laughed suddenly. "But guess
what. The drawings are all over the news.
They're not saying how they were found,
but they've had all these experts look at
them already, and it's such a big deal.
Everyone on TV is so excited. They had an
interview with one of the German guys from
that museum where the other two were

stolen, and he kept saying something like 'Wunderbar! Wunderbar!' My dad says that means 'wonderful.' "

Marvin thought that it must be a dream come true for the museum people, to have all four of Dürer's long-lost *Virtues* returned in one fell swoop.

James lifted Marvin close to his face, grinning at him. "And it's all because of us! Well, you, mostly. But I helped. And Christina says they've gotten permission to put all of the drawings in some special exhibit, before they have to send them back. So they hung them this morning, and Dad just called and he says the lines for the museum are around the block. We're going to go, all of us, this afternoon! Isn't that great?"

James let out a long breath. "So you have to come, too, of course. You're like a real, live hero!" He set Marvin down, looking at him proudly. "Nobody will ever know. But you are."

That's okay, Marvin thought. *You know.*

As scary as it had been at times, the whole adventure had been something to share with James. It was a secret kept between them.

JAMES'S GIFT

It was a strange little group that walked into the Met's Drawings and Prints Gallery late that afternoon to see the newly reunited Dürer miniatures. Escorted by a museum guard, who had greeted them at a side entrance so that they could avoid the crowds, Karl, James (with Marvin tucked securely under his jacket cuff, having sworn to Mama and Papa that he wouldn't budge from that position for the entire outing), and Mr. and Mrs. Pompaday, pushing William in his stroller, waited for Christina at the front of the exhibit.

Though she'd heard only the minimal details of the drawings' recovery, Mrs.

Pompaday could barely contain her pride over her son's involvement — even in what she imagined was an ancillary fashion. She kept patting James's back importantly and looking around for reporters.

"I wonder if anyone will interview you, James. They certainly ought to! Of course, once this business with the museum is behind us, I expect you to get back to work on your own pictures. That's where the real opportunity is. Four thousand from the Mortons! Just think what other people will pay for your extraordinary drawings."

Mr. Pompaday harrumphed in agreement. "I've got a couple of partners at work who might be interested. Quite a way to build your college fund, James."

Marvin winced, while James's freckled cheeks turned a dark pink. "I don't know if I'm going to keep drawing those little pictures," he said. "They take a lot of time."

"What do you mean?" his mother cried. "They're marvelous! You can't stop, James. Why, that's your gift."

"I know, but I was thinking I could do bigger drawings —"

"No, no, no," his mother protested. "It's their little size that makes them so delightful."

Marvin inwardly groaned. How would he

and James ever stop this charade? He couldn't go on forging pictures. Just look at the trouble this had gotten them into already . . . even if it had led to the return of the stolen drawings.

Karl interrupted them. "Maybe he wants to take a break from it for a while. All artists need that occasionally."

"Oh, I don't think so —" Mrs. Pompaday began.

"My friends!" Christina cried happily, appearing in the doorway.

After the necessary introductions — "You have a remarkable son," she told Mrs. Pompaday, who nodded smugly — Christina led them through the crush of visitors to the third room, where the Dürer *Virtue* drawings were prominently displayed along one wall. Marvin clung to James's wrist and peered up, trying to see them better.

Matted and framed, they were imposing despite their tiny size. Seeing them together somehow made you look at each drawing more closely, Marvin thought, instinctively comparing the four figures. Fortitude looked more determined and courageous, Justice both sterner and sadder alongside her sisters.

They were breathtaking. *Nobody can draw like Dürer,* Marvin thought, *not even me.* He

suddenly and purely hoped that he wouldn't have to copy any more drawings. He was tired of it. He wanted to make something of his own.

"I've noticed details I never saw before," Christina said excitedly. "The line of Prudence's jaw, the way Justice's hand rests here. It's as if the drawings speak to one another."

Karl smiled at her. "They were meant to hang together," he said. "You can tell."

"They certainly make a nice arrangement," Mrs. Pompaday added, not to be outdone. "James, you should consider doing a group of miniatures like this. It would be fetching, really." She turned to Christina. "He has a gift, you know," she confided.

"Oh, I know," Christina said, smiling at James.

He does have a gift, Marvin wanted to say. *It's just not what you think it is.*

"This exhibit is going to bring new attention to Dürer," Christina continued. "I can feel it. Museum admissions today are at a record high already. We've had dozens of calls from the media. The return of the drawings is getting international news coverage. I think Dürer may finally get the interest he deserves!"

As the others continued to admire the drawings, James tugged her aside. "What about Denny?" he asked anxiously. "Do the police know where he is?"

Christina shook her head. "They're watching the airports in Germany. Nothing yet."

"Do you think they'll catch him?"

Christina pursed her lips. "I don't know, James."

"I hope they don't," James said. "I like Denny."

"I do too." Christina sighed.

James watched her soberly. "Do you think he's mad at me?" he asked.

"Oh, no, James, I don't think so," she answered firmly. "I think that, wherever he is, he must be relieved in a way. Even though things didn't turn out as he'd planned, at least it's over." She tilted her head, looking at the four miniatures. "It's like when you tell a lie and then you have to tell more lies because of it, to cover it up. Have you ever done that? And even if it's horrible and embarrassing to be caught, it's also a relief at some level . . . you know? Because then you can stop doing this thing you wished you'd never done in the first place."

James looked at her. "Yeah. I know what you mean," he said finally.

Marvin knew he was thinking about his own drawings. It was so complicated and exhausting to keep up the ruse of James's artistic genius. And when would it end?

"So," Christina continued, "I think Denny is probably grateful to you. Or maybe he isn't right now, but he will be."

"Will we ever see him again?"

Christina paused. "I don't know. He committed a serious crime. If he shows up here in the States, he'll be put in jail. And I know the FBI agents have been talking to the German police to see if they can link him to the other thefts."

James bit his lip. "I wish he didn't have to go to jail."

"I know," Christina said softly.

"Well, this is a very impressive exhibit,"

Mrs. Pompaday interjected, coming to their side. "But we've made reservations at a little French place on the Upper West Side and we really should be going. It was nice to meet you, Ms. Balcony."

"And you," Christina said. "Thank you for loaning me your wonderful son."

"Oh, my, I was glad for him to have lessons with you. It's been a very special opportunity for James."

Christina smiled quizzically. "I don't think there's much I could teach James."

She escorted them to the museum exit, and as Mr. and Mrs. Pompaday navigated the long flight of stairs with William's stroller, she turned to Karl.

"Thank you," she said. "For all of your help. It was really lovely getting to know you two."

"Won't we see you again?" James asked, looking crushed. Marvin felt a similar wave of disappointment. He hadn't even considered that they'd be saying good-bye to Christina.

"Oh, of course!" Christina said. "Any time you like. I hope you'll keep in touch." She rested her hand on Karl's arm.

He looked at her, and Marvin saw his face turn the same shade of pink that James's did when he was embarrassed about something. "Maybe we could get a cup of coffee sometime?" he asked hesitantly.

Christina smiled. "Absolutely. I'd like that."

"Good, I'll call you," Karl said over his shoulder, ushering James down the steps after the Pompadays.

When they reached the sidewalk, he bent and kissed the top of James's head. "Love you, buddy."

"Yeah, Dad," James said. "You too."

"We'll do something on Wednesday, okay?"

Mrs. Pompaday interrupted. "We'll see, Karl. James may need that time to work on a few new pieces."

James squirmed, while Karl looked at him sympathetically. "Okay, we'll talk later," he said. He ruffled James's hair, then headed off down the sidewalk.

At the curb, Mr. Pompaday hailed a cab. William began to howl. He arched his back in protest, kicking the footrest of the stroller.

"Oh, sweetheart," Mrs. Pompaday crooned. "Yes, yes, you're hungry. We're going now." She unstrapped him from the seat and thrust him into Mr. Pompaday's arms, calling, "James, put his stroller in the trunk, will you?"

As James folded the stroller and handed it

344

to the cabbie, Marvin felt him hesitate. It was only for a second, but in that fraction of time, Marvin went rigid. *No, James!* he thought, sensing what was about to happen even before he consciously understood it.

He saw James's right hand reach toward the open trunk at the exact same moment that the cabbie slammed the trunk closed.

There was a sickening, thwarted clunk as

the metal trunk crashed down on something
that wasn't meant to be there. And an
anguished cry.

James stumbled backward, sobbing in
pain, holding his right hand.

No, no, no, Marvin thought, the word
pounding in his head, as he gripped James's
other wrist.

"James!" Mrs. Pompaday screamed.

MASTERPIECE

It was on a sunny winter afternoon several days later that Marvin crawled out of the family home and found a little scrap of paper behind the wastebasket, with a shaky black X on it. His heart leapt. He hadn't seen James since his injury. There had been such a commotion that day: a frantic cab ride to the hospital, James bravely trying to hold back tears, the Pompadays loudly blaming themselves and each other for asking him to put William's stroller in the trunk. ("What if his hand doesn't recover? What if he can't draw again? I shall never forgive myself! Never!" Mrs. Pompaday had vowed.) Then, at the hospital, Marvin had been forced to hold on for dear life as the jacket was tossed aside, and James's hand was examined and X-rayed and wrapped in a cast.

"Is the damage permanent?" Mrs. Pompaday had demanded anxiously of every doctor who passed through the room.

"It's a bad break," one doctor said. "But with physical therapy, he should be fine."

"No, no, you don't understand," Mrs. Pompaday persisted. "My son is an artist, a very talented one. He does these wonderful little miniature drawings —"

The doctor cut her off. "We'll have to wait and see how it heals."

Back home again, Marvin endlessly replayed the scene on the street in his head. Had James done it on purpose? There was no way to know. But when he told Mama and Papa his suspicions, they were appalled.

"Of course he didn't deliberately break his own hand!" Mama cried. "James would never do such a thing."

"Besides, who knows how that injury will affect the use of his hand?" Papa added. "Forget the drawings; what if James can't throw a baseball again? Or write his name properly? He's too smart a boy to take that kind of risk."

Marvin hoped his parents were right, but

he was not so sure. He knew how desperate James had been to stop faking a talent he didn't have.

Marvin had visited James's bedroom often over the past few days, but he had somehow always managed to miss him. He'd even lingered under the kitchen table during the Pompadays' dinner, just to listen to James describe the reaction of the kids at school to his broken hand and to the tale of the stolen drawings. Apparently, they'd crowded around him, full of questions and compliments. They'd squabbled over a chance to sign the cast. They wanted to sit with him at lunchtime. Marvin hoped the whole thing would make James a celebrity for a while. It would be good for James to have more human friends.

But not ONLY human friends, Marvin thought, feeling lonesome for him. They hadn't seen each other in days and days, after spending so much time together. It wasn't even the amount of time, it was the intensity of it — so much had happened to the two of them. Marvin felt changed by it, and he knew James was the only one who could really understand that.

"What's the matter, darling?" his mother asked him one evening.

"I miss James," Marvin said. "Do you

think he's forgotten about me?"

"Oh, no, darling, of course not! I know he hasn't. Come with me. I have something to show you."

Taking him gently by the leg, Mama led him through the living room to the narrow hallway that connected their home with the home of Albert, Edith, and Elaine. Marvin could see a new opening in the wall of the corridor.

"What's that?" he asked.

"Look inside," Mama said, smiling.

Marvin caught his breath. Through the doorway was a new room, freshly hollowed out. White plaster dust sifted lightly onto the floor. In the center was a small bottle cap filled with ink, covered with a tiny sheet of plastic wrap. Several small, torn scraps of paper were stacked next to it.

"Mama! What is this place?" Marvin cried.

His mother beamed at him. "A studio, darling — a real artist's studio, just for you! Your father and Uncle Albert have been working on it all day. And where do you suppose the ink and paper came from?"

Marvin knew.

"He left them in the cupboard yesterday. Even covered the ink with plastic wrap so it will last longer. . . . Isn't he a clever, thoughtful boy?" Mama hugged him. "This

way, you can draw whenever you like. And whatever you like, Marvin."

Marvin's heart felt big enough to burst his shell.

The next day, Marvin was thrilled to spy the piece of paper with the X on it in the corner of the cupboard. He scurried to James's bedroom at a little before four o'clock. James was lying on his bed, reading, with his cast propped awkwardly at an angle. As Marvin crossed the tedious expanse of rug, he noticed with satisfaction that James kept sneaking glances at the top of his desk. Of course James hadn't forgotten him! *He's been watching for me,* Marvin thought.

"Oh!" he heard James cry. "There you are, little guy! Let me give you a ride." He leapt off the bed and plunked his cast in front of Marvin, grinning.

"What do you think?" he demanded. "It's pretty great, huh?" The white of the cast was obscured by colorful Magic Marker signatures and doodles. "I got everybody in my class to sign, and about half of Mrs. Kellogg's class too. They love this thing."

Marvin clambered onto the cast, and James lifted him up. "Did you get the ink? And the paper? I checked and it was gone, so I guess you did. That way you can keep drawing! And when you need more ink, just leave the cap out in the cupboard and I'll refill it. Okay?"

Marvin smiled up at him.

James carried him across the room. "I wanted you to come 'cause I have something to show you," he announced, barely able to hide his excitement. He walked toward the bedroom wall and stopped a few feet away, holding his cast aloft. "Look!"

There, in front of them, was Marvin's drawing of the street, beautifully matted and framed. It hung next to the window, a tiny replica of the outdoor scene with its street-lamp and tree and rooftop.

Marvin stared at it. This was the drawing

he thought James had sold. To the Mortons,
for four thousand dollars. How could it be
here, in his room, hanging on the wall like a
real picture? Like something that could be
in a museum.

"Doesn't it look great?" James continued
happily. "Christina framed it for me. And
guess what. She's going to frame your *Forti-*

tude, too, and give it to me. She said it was the least she could do after all my help." He grinned at Marvin. "All our help."

Marvin looked at James in amazement. He'd get to see *Fortitude* again, too! He couldn't wait to show it to Mama and Papa and all of the relatives.

James rested his cast on the wall next to the picture so that Marvin was only inches away from his little cityscape. "You're surprised, right? You thought we sold it. And we were supposed to, but after what happened to my hand, my mom couldn't do it. She's all worried I'll never be able to make another one. And" — he smiled — "I won't."

James flexed his fingers and studied the cast. "Wow, did that hurt! But it worked out okay in the end. You and me, we couldn't keep making those little drawings, you know? I wish there'd been a way to tell everybody the truth. But it was too hard. And I was afraid of what they might do to you . . . you know?"

Marvin looked up at James, filled with a warm tide of something he'd never felt before. It was more than happiness. More than affection or gratitude. It was something deeper. It was the sense of being seen and loved exactly for who he was.

Not the way his parents loved him, which was as steady and certain as the streetlamp shining outside James's window each night. This was different: the feeling of being chosen. Out of everybody in the world, Marvin realized, this boy had picked him as the one he liked best of all.

"Anyway," James was saying, "my mom decided we couldn't sell it because it might be my last great masterpiece and we have to hold on to it. She wanted to put it in the living room, of course, because that way more people would see it."

He laughed. "But it looks good here, don't you think? It's like having another window in the wall . . . a really tiny one. And you know what? If *you* had a little bedroom in this same spot, next to mine, this is what you'd see from *your* window."

Marvin smiled. It was true. It was James's window in miniature, the perfect scale for a beetle.

"You'll never guess what I'm doing to-night," James said, carrying Marvin over to his desk and setting his cast gently on the wood. Marvin climbed down and looked at him expectantly. "I'm having dinner with my dad" — James paused, grinning — "and Christina! They're taking me out for pizza." He lowered his voice conspiratorially. "I think my dad likes her."

Karl and Christina. That fits, Marvin thought. It would be like a second family for James . . . a different, artistic family.

James laughed suddenly. "You know something? You're my best friend. Isn't that funny?"

Marvin beamed up at him.

A great friendship was like a great work of art, he thought. It took time and attention, and a spark of something that was impossible to describe. It was a happy, lucky accident, finding some kindred part of yourself in a total stranger.

There was a knock on the door, and Marvin heard Karl's voice.

"I have to go now," James told him, setting him gently on the desk. "Dad's here. But I'll see you tomorrow. Or I'll check for the X behind the wastebasket!"

He got his jacket from the closet and waved at Marvin. "Bye, little guy."

Marvin lifted one of his legs and waved it in response.

When the room was empty, he crawled to the edge of the desk and looked out the window. He thought of all the things he and James could do together when spring came. They could take long walks. They could go to the park. They could visit the Met with

Karl and Christina, and then Marvin could come back to his little studio and make pictures of his own.

Marvin smiled to himself. There was a whole wide world waiting to be explored, and there was nobody he'd rather do it with than James.

AUTHOR'S NOTE

ABOUT THE ART

In this story, all of the background information about Albrecht Dürer and his contemporaries is true, but Dürer's four *Virtue* drawings are purely a figment of my imagination. Dürer did complete several miniature drawings, in ink, with the level of detail described here. He was also a long-standing admirer of the Italian Renaissance artist Giovanni Bellini, who did a miniature drawing *Fortitude* (the girl wrestling the lion), which is indeed held by the J. Paul Getty Museum in California and is described in this story. It is reproduced below.

ABOUT THE THEFT

Except for the thefts of my fictional *Virtue* drawings, all of the art heists described in the book really happened, and there is a special FBI unit focused on the recovery of

Giovanni Bellini, Fortitude, *about 1470. Pen and brown ink, approximately 3.5 inches square*

Courtesy J. Paul Getty Museum, Los Angeles

stolen art. However, for understandable reasons, art museums and law-enforcement agencies are very reluctant to share information about their security practices. The details in this story concerning the theft of *Fortitude* from the Met and the FBI procedures involved are purely fictional.

ABOUT THE BEETLES

Marvin and his family are intended to be a kind of ground beetle, of which there are more than two thousand varieties. Their life span can be as long as three or four years,

Dürer, Stag Beetle, *1505*
Courtesy J. Paul Getty Museum, Los Angeles

and though they generally live outdoors, they sometimes wander indoors and remain. Most species don't fly. They eat a variety of foods and tend to be more active at night.

ACKNOWLEDGMENTS

In a book about friendship, it is a particular pleasure to thank the following people who are such an important part of my life: my editor, Christy Ottaviano, whose careful eye and thoughtful insights have immeasurably improved my work; my sister, Mary Broach, who has a gift for responding to a manuscript as a parent, former kid, and critic simultaneously; and my enormously talented, far-flung group of readers, who are also wonderful friends — Jane Burns, Claire Carlson, Laura Forte, Jane Kamensky, Jill Lepore, and Carol Sheriff. I am very lucky to have them.

I am also grateful to several young readers and listeners — Jane and Margaret Urheim, and Gideon and Simon Leek — for their helpful reactions to a draft of this book. Special thanks to Caroline Meckler for sharing her knowledge of the Metropolitan Museum of Art, and to the staff at Holt for doing such a fine job of ushering my books into the world.

Finally, a big and endless thank-you to my family — my husband, Ward Wheeler, and my children, Zoe, Harry, and Grace — for their flexibility, enthusiasm, and support. Years ago at a Chinese restaurant, the fortune in my fortune cookie read: "Your family is one of nature's masterpieces." I believe it.

ABOUT THE AUTHOR AND THE ILLUSTRATOR

Elise Broach is the author of the acclaimed novels *Shakespeare's Secret* and *Desert Crossing*. The idea for *Masterpiece* started when she lost a contact lens down the bathroom sink. She sat on the tile floor for an hour trying to get the pipe loose to no avail and fantasized about how wonderful it would be if a tiny creature could go fetch it. She wrote the first few chapters of the story that night and then didn't return to it for twenty years. Elise holds undergraduate and graduate degrees in history from Yale University. She lives with her family in Easton, Connecticut.

www.elisebroach.com

Kelly Murphy has illustrated many books for children including *Hush, Little Dragon*. She lives in North Attleboro, Massachusetts.

www.kelmurphy.com

The employees of Thorndike Press hope you have enjoyed this Large Print book. All our Thorndike and Wheeler Large Print titles are designed for easy reading, and all our books are made to last. Other Thorndike Press Large Print books are available at your library, through selected bookstores, or directly from us.

For information about titles, please call:
(800) 223-1244

or visit our Web site at:
http://gale.cengage.com/thorndike

To share your comments, please write:
Publisher
Thorndike Press
295 Kennedy Memorial Drive
Waterville, ME 04901